DRAGONS OF KILAUEA

A KATHY WEST NATIONAL PARK ADVENTURE

RUSSELL JAMES

SEVERED PRESS
HOBART TASMANIA

DRAGONS OF KILAUEA

Copyright © 2020 Russell James

WWW.SEVEREDPRESS.COM

All rights reserved. No part of this book may be
reproduced or transmitted in any form or by any
electronic or mechanical means, including
photocopying, recording or by any information and
retrieval system, without the written permission of
the publisher and author, except where permitted by law.
This novel is a work of fiction. Names,
characters, places and incidents are the product of
the author's imagination, or are used fictitiously.
Any resemblance to actual events, locales or persons,
living or dead, is purely coincidental.

ISBN: 978-1-922323-90-3

All rights reserved.

Other books by Russell James

Dedication

For Denise, Maria, and all the other members of the National Park Service who endure hardship and sacrifice to preserve the history and habitats of this great nation.

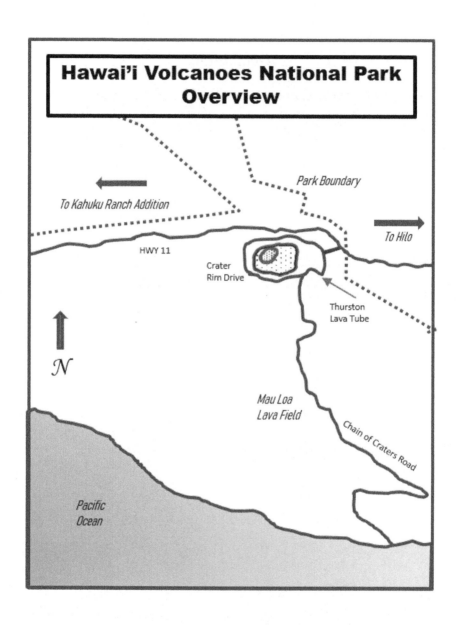

Hawai'i Volcanoes National Park Overview

Park Boundary

To Kahuku Ranch Addition

To Hilo

HWY 11

Crater
Rim Drive

Thurston
Lava Tube

𝒩

Mau Loa
Lava Field

Chain of Craters Road

Pacific
Ocean

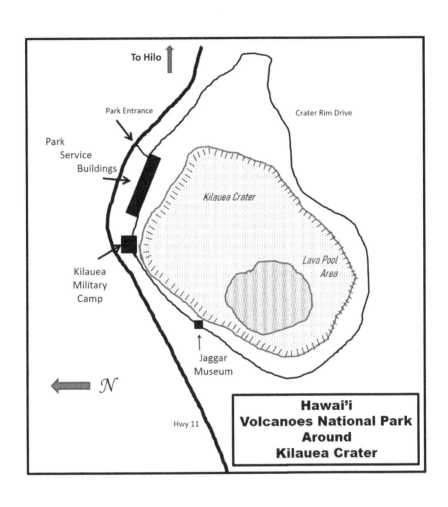

To Hilo

Park Entrance

Crater Rim Drive

Park
Service
Buildings

Kilauea Crater

*Lava Pool
Area*

Kilauea
Military
Camp

Jaggar
Museum

𝒩

Hwy 11

**Hawai'i
Volcanoes National Park
Around
Kilauea Crater**

CHAPTER 1

Sammy Yun woke up with a hangover. After every night of serious drinking, his pounding head and parched throat always came as a surprise. He thought whatever god delivered this agonizing retribution for his transgressions would eventually discover it ineffective, and give up. Today apparently wasn't that day.

The short, rotund man staggered out of bed and tossed on the red, thrift store kimono that drew duty as his bathrobe. Arriving in the cluttered kitchen, he mixed his patented hot sauce and pickle juice hangover cure. Sammy washed down a double dosage of pain reliever with the concoction and then padded over to the sliding glass door. He took a deep breath, braced himself, and opened the drapes.

Hawaiian sunshine blasted Sammy's face like a *Star Trek* phaser and seemed to light his eyes on fire. He shielded himself with one hand and stepped out onto his deck and into the humid tropical air.

His house was off the beaten path, out of town along the edge of Volcanoes National Park, southwest of Hilo. The small, wooden bungalow had been built against a steep, long-dormant section of Kilauea, and the building sat on a series of staggered stilts that topped out about six feet high downslope. Lush, green vegetation threatened to subjugate the abode. When he wasn't selling T-shirts to tourists, Sammy's never-ending chore was keeping just ahead of the onslaught. As with many things, he was currently behind on that task.

He pulled a cigarette from the pack in the kimono sleeve and lit it up. He exhaled a cloud of smoke.

Under the house, something stirred.

Wild pigs were his first thought. The non-indigenous bastards were notorious for making a mess of yards and gardens when they decided it was time to go rooting. Fencing in the area under the house was one of those projects he was behind on.

He slipped on a pair of flip flops and grabbed the tattered golf umbrella he kept by the stairs for occasions that called for pig-threatening. Pointing it at them while popping it open and closed scared off the smaller ones. Nothing scared the bigger ones. He teetered down the steps to see which size hog he faced.

At the foot of the steps he looked under the deck and saw nothing. The lower level of sunlight had kept the vegetation at ankle-length here, and closer to the house the slope turned to stark, black volcanic basalt. If a pig had been there, it had high-tailed it.

Traces of sulphur wafted through the air. His initial fear was a leak from his natural gas tank, but that was on the other side of the house. That left the option of it being a gift from Kilauea. Hissing steam vents popped up all over the island when the volcano got active. It just hadn't been active here in forever. If the volcano had awakened, he could kiss his house goodbye.

He walked under the deck and began to sweep across the weeds with his umbrella. Active vents sometimes released little steam, but plenty of scalding air. Even though there wasn't the usual telltale blackened vegetation that surrounded such vents, he wasn't going to take any chance of stepping into one of those little portals to Hell. After minutes of searching, he found neither pig nor vent.

He stopped at the basalt wall under the house. The sulphurous scent was much stronger. He looked closely and saw a ten-centimeter hole in the rock. Sammy couldn't remember the last time he poked around down here, but he was certain there hadn't been any holes. And field mice might get in the trash, but they weren't up for digging into solid rock.

He took a sniff near the hole. Definitely the sulphur source. He flashed his hand across it. No heat. That was good. He wondered if it was a hole or just a crack in the stone.

He poked the folded umbrella through the hole. No resistance. He angled the umbrella around in a circle. It seemed like there was a lot of open space on the other side of the opening.

Suddenly, the umbrella tugged in Sammy's hand, as if something on the other side had grabbed it. It jerked out of his grip and disappeared into the hole.

"What the hell?"

Sammy bent down and peered into the darkness.

The wall of rock exploded. Stones struck him in the head and the impact sent him flying. He landed on his back and saw stars.

His vision cleared. A leathery, narrow face looked down on him. A massive head filled his field of view. Dark gray, pebbled skin stretched over a long snout. Breath puffed from its twin nostrils and blanketed him in the stench of rotten eggs. The malevolent, solid black eyes of a giant dragon stared him down.

Sammy screamed and tried to crawl backwards. A red, forked tongue whipped from the dragon's mouth and slapped him across the face. His cheek burned. Saliva dripped from the corner of the creature's mouth and dropped onto Sammy's exposed bare leg. His skin sizzled and Sammy wailed and beat his hands against his searing skin.

The dragon roared, a high-pitched shriek like shearing metal. Then it exhaled and coated the underside of the wooden deck in a stream of liquid fire.

Fast as a bolt of lightning, its head darted down. Its jaws snapped shut around Sammy's neck. Sammy's decapitated body hit the ground as the dragon swallowed his head.

CHAPTER 2

Ranger Kathy West knelt and checked the tread depth on the over-sized tires of the black Jeep Wrangler. They still had plenty of life. She hoped the rest of the vehicle could say the same. The miles were low and the truck didn't look like it had spent much time off-road. The soft top was folded back so the Hawaiian sun beat down on the tan leather seats. But they looked good as new, more evidence of light past usage.

"That's a nice one," said a man behind her.

She turned on the balls of her feet to see a short man wearing a Hawaiian shirt. It bulged over his beer belly. Long, scraggly hair framed a face uncharacteristically pasty for a used car salesman living in the tropics.

"That Jeep might be a bit much for a lady, though," he said. "I have a VW Beetle that might suit you."

Kathy rolled her eyes. She stood to her full height of nearly six feet and looked down on the insect of a man. Her short, blonde hair was in a tight pony tail and she wore a Volcanoes National Park T-shirt and tapered cargo pants. Her military-style backpack sat at her feet.

The salesman managed a nervous smile and took a step back. Even out of her Park Service uniform, Kathy could manage to be intimidating.

"'Course that Jeep might be the right thing for you after all," he said. "Got a trade in?"

"Nope."

Kathy's last assignment had been at Fort Jefferson in the Dry Tortugas, an island many miles off the coast of Key West, Florida. No need for a vehicle there. It probably wouldn't have survived that tour of duty, anyway.

"Well, I can get you a nice financing rate, put you in this for about $600 a month."

That was a stupid price for this vehicle. She looked around the lot. A fine soot from the Kilauea volcano's random out-gasses covered all the cars. Most were much older than this Jeep. The cheap, colored pennants that fluttered near the office door had ragged edges. It looked like the recent spate of eruptions had pushed this guy's business to a financial brink. She might have *wanted* to buy a car today, but he *needed* to sell one.

"Here's a counter offer." Kathy pulled out a roll of cash. She counted out hundred dollar bills onto the hood of the Jeep until they tallied the vehicle's wholesale value. "I hand you this, you sign over the title."

The salesman laughed. "I can't let this nice ride go for that little. I'll need five hundred more than that."

Kathy took one of the hundreds and put it back in her pocket. "The offer is now this much."

"What? Are you crazy? That's not how you negotiate."

"I'm not negotiating." She took another hundred off the pile. "The offer is now this much."

The salesman's eyes bulged. He stared at the pile of money. His eyes danced back and forth, as if he was doing some kind of math comparing what he'd paid for the Jeep and what overdue bills sat on his desk.

Kathy reached for another hundred.

"Okay! Okay!" he said. "You have a deal."

Kathy shouldered her backpack and he led her into the office. Twenty minutes later Kathy walked out of the office carrying a title and a set of keys. She tossed her pack in the back of the Jeep and sat in the front seat.

Her time at isolated Fort Jefferson had allowed her to save most of her paycheck, and she just dumped a chunk of that savings into this truck. But she had to do it. She needed transportation that could go anywhere during this new assignment to Volcanoes National Park on the Big Island, as the locals called the island of Hawaii. The park encompassed 323,000 acres of land, and most of the roads were not improved.

She fired up the Jeep, slid the gearshift into first, and eased out of the used car lot. She chugged through the downtown Hilo traffic for a bit until she made it to the bay. Under the clear sky, the water practically glowed an amazing shade of blue. Palm trees stretched skyward and their fronds waved lazily in the onshore breeze. She stayed on the shoreline road and then turned right for the long uphill drive on Hawaii Route 11 to Volcanoes National Park.

On paper, she had a routine re-assignment as a ranger in the park. But after the events at Fort Jefferson, no assignment she'd ever get would be routine.

At Fort Jefferson, she and Ranger Nathan Toland had battled rogue CIA agents and an army of giant crabs the men planned on unleashing on the American mainland. In the end they'd saved the day, but had to go to Washington, D.C. headquarters to answer for all the damage done to the park. Once there, they were recruited by Deputy Director Cynthia Leister to become undercover agents for a shadowy section of the National Park

Service. The job of that section was to keep the various supernatural phenomena in the National Park system at bay. She and Nathan's cryptic reassignment to Volcanoes NP had come with no details about what she might find at the park.

The temperature cooled as the road's elevation increased. She was about to pull over and put up the soft top when the entrance sign to the park appeared. She turned right off the highway and into the park entrance.

The park headquarters building was adjacent to the visitor's center and the two buildings were completely different. While the state-of-the-art visitor's center had sweeping glass windows and a very modern look, the simple, rectangular headquarters building looked the same as when it had been built in the 1930s. Par for the course for the Park Service. The priority was always on the park's guests. And Kathy was fine with that.

Kathy entered the headquarters building. A sign read that Superintendent Bradley Butler's office was at the end of the hall. She stopped outside his open door. Butler stood behind his desk reading something in a file folder. He was a few inches shorter than Kathy and bulged a bit in his Park Service uniform, like middle-aged spread was getting the best of him. He had a bushy, gray, walrus-type moustache.

Kathy stepped over to his desk. "Kathy West, reporting in."

Butler looked up and then shook her hand. "West? Great! Good to get some reinforcements."

Butler sat down behind his desk and Kathy took a seat facing him.

"We've been short-handed just as the number of visitors has spiked," Butler said. "Kilauea's recent eruptions have been a big draw."

Kilauea was the active volcano at the heart of the park. Eruptions over the last year had buried hundreds of acres outside the park under slow-moving lava flows. National news had been all over it.

"I'd think that an active volcano would keep visitors away."

"We were closed for a while," Butler said. "The volcano was blasting boulders out of the caldera during the eruption's peak. Eventually, Kilauea calmed down. As soon as we reopened, cars were lined up down Highway 11. People want to see lava."

"Can they?"

Butler went over to the park map on the wall. The volcano's caldera was a large, irregular circle in the center, surrounded by a service road and several campgrounds. The active vent was designated by a wide red circle on the west side of the caldera. He pointed to the Jaggar Museum Visitor's Center on the caldera's northwest section.

"Visitors can drive this far," he said. "There they can see the lava pool from a safe distance. But west of that, and in fact the western third of the caldera, is closed to the public."

"Do you get pushback from visitors who want to get closer? The lava pool is hundreds of feet below the caldera's rim. It's not like it's going to bubble up and splatter people."

"You know how it is," Butler said. "People think a National Park is as safe as a theme park. It isn't. We have to explain that the threat is from the poisonous gasses the vents give off. A shift in the wind could send an invisible, toxic plume up the caldera's western side. Visitors couldn't get out of the way fast enough."

"How's the activity since last year's eruptions?"

"Much calmer. The underground magma levels have dropped significantly. But most of the activity was outside the park boundaries anyway. The lava traveled through underground fissures and flowed out of vents at the volcano's base. The geologists say the worst is behind us and we'll be entering into another calm period."

Kathy thought that was good news. Whatever supernatural event had triggered her reassignment here, she didn't need a natural disaster piled on top of it.

"Glad that threat has passed."

"But there is another. Invasive species. That's where I'll need you and your scientific background."

Kathy had done her research. The Hawaiian Islands had been a closed system until the first Hawaiians arrived. From then on it had been a constant battle to keep hardier foreign species from outcompeting indigenous populations. Some intruders were animals like pigs and rats. Others were plants like kahili ginger.

"I have local volunteers and junior rangers to do the outreach work with the visitors," Butler continued. "I'll be expecting you to check some of the less traveled trails, recording and rooting out the invasive species. We can't let them get a critical mass, or we'll never get ahead of them."

Kathy remembered the giant crabs that overran Fort Jefferson. That was kind of the ultimate invasive species. Compared to that, uprooting non-native flowers along hiking trails was going to be, literally, a walk in the park.

Butler pulled a set of keys from his desk drawer and handed them to Kathy. "You're in Cabin Four in Ranger Housing. Cozy, but clean. It certainly beats paying for an apartment in Hilo, especially with everyone the lava displaced. Go ahead and get yourself moved in today and you can start work tomorrow."

"Sounds good."

Butler leaned back in his chair and steepled his fingers. "A few things I want to clear up before you get to work."

This was the discussion Kathy had dreaded. She faked a smile. "Fire away."

"You were in charge of Dry Tortugas," Butler said. "You're not in charge here. Is that going to be a problem?"

"Not at all. This is a much bigger park. You have the level of experience needed to run it, I don't."

That was a load of crap. Kathy knew she could run the park, and probably better than Butler did. But part of her deal with Deputy Director Leister was that her visible career was going to go into a holding pattern. She'd be taking lower-level positions to keep a lower profile, and to give her more time to work on her clandestine project, keeping the world safe from the monsters some National Parks protected the world from.

"And I did a little more checking," Butler said. "Fort Jefferson was temporarily closed under your watch."

"Storm damage made the dock and some of the fort structure unsafe. We got it all put back together."

Actually, it had been giant crabs and automatic weapons fire that had made the old fort unsafe for visitors. But Deputy Director Leister had concocted the storm damage cover story for the rest of the organization and the world beyond.

"Well, I'll expect more proactive efforts here," Butler said. "We have hurricanes just like Florida but with the right planning we can keep any damage to a minimum."

Kathy would have loved to ask this little man what action plan he'd have had in place for an attack by crabs the size of Cadillacs, but she couldn't share any of that story with anyone.

"Sure thing," she said.

Butler rose and shook her hand again. "Excellent. See you at seven in the morning tomorrow and we'll get you started."

Kathy left the headquarters building, glad to be able to avoid any more questions about her last assignment. She was ready to settle into her new quarters, but she had one thing to do first.

She stopped by the visitor center and checked the ranger interpretation schedule. She ran her finger down the list. She stopped at one called *The Civilian Conservation Corps at Kilauea*. It was being held at the Jaggar Museum in less than an hour.

She had a pretty good idea who'd be leading that talk. Nathan's area of specialization was history.

CHAPTER 3

The Jaggar Museum stood a few miles down Crater Rim Road. With the road beyond it closed, it had become the last stop. The modernist structure stood near the crater's edge, with a wide natural stone patio that overlooked the lava pool at the floor of the caldera. Kathy parked her Jeep and made her way across the parking lot to the museum entrance. She didn't need to go inside to find the ranger giving the history talk. Ranger Nathan Toland stood beside one of the binocular telescopes at the patio's walled edge. Ten tourists stood around him in a half circle.

The crisp NPS uniform and wide-brimmed campaign hat could not disguise that Nathan was a slight and geeky twenty-something. Bushy, dark hair framed sparkling brown eyes. Around his neck hung a necklace of large, polished brown nuts. He'd arrived two weeks earlier, while Kathy was getting her replacement at the restored Fort Jefferson up to speed. He flashed an infectious smile as he showed the group a black-and-white picture of men in T-shirts quarrying stone.

"So at the height of the Depression," he said, "the CCC brought a platoon of men in here and they began to quarry rocks from older lava flows. Those rocks built a host of projects like retaining walls, a dam, and a variety of buildings. You're standing on some of them right now."

Everyone looked down at their feet.

"That infusion of labor helped turn what was an inaccessible park into the improved and highly visited park you see today, a crown jewel in our great National Park system. So remember all the effort those men put into this place, and make sure that you leave the park just as you found it when you arrived. Haul out all your trash, stick to the walking trails, and leave all plants and animals for the next visitor to see."

The crowd offered up a smattering of applause and drifted away. Nathan gathered up his photos and then noticed Kathy. He broke out into a big smile as she approached.

"Hardly recognize you out of uniform and not being attacked by giant crabs," he said.

Kathy gave him a quick hug, then gave the lei of nuts around his neck a poke.

"What's with these?"

"Kukui nuts," he said. "In Hawaiian culture, they symbolize that I am a bearer of light."

Nathan had a penchant for historical immersion at his assignment, even if it ended up being as uncomfortable as the woolen underwear he'd tried at Fort Jefferson.

"I just checked in with Butler," Kathy said.

"He's okay. Kind of a bureaucrat, but he keeps the wheels turning."

"He talked to me about Fort Jefferson but didn't mention you were here."

"My tour at Fort Jefferson has been expunged from the records," Nathan said, "just like Deputy Director Leister said it would. As far as everyone here knows, I spent the last few months in Acadia National Park. And the two of us are meeting for the first time."

"That's good. It would seem suspicious if we both came from the same place at the same time." Kathy looked around to confirm that no one was within earshot. "Any clue why we've been transferred here?"

"An awesome reward for saving Florida from giant crabs?"

"Doubt it."

"Then, no. Nothing out of the ordinary has been going on here. Busy. But the volcano has settled back to just bubbling and there hasn't been anything alarming going on."

"I'm going to go move in. I'm in Quarters Four."

"I'm in Six. Come by tonight and dinner's on me."

"Something Hawaiian, I assume."

"Totally."

Given Nathan's history of sampling almost any food, his answer made her very nervous.

***

Later that night, Kathy sat at the dining room table in Quarters Six, nervously awaiting whatever strange entrée Nathan was going to foist on her. He'd steadfastly refused to give her any hints.

"Ready or not," Nathan called from the kitchen, "here it comes."

Kathy braced herself as Nathan approached the table with two plates in hand. He placed one in front of Kathy. The meal consisted of broiled fish and a mix of zucchini, cherry tomatoes, and red peppers. Kathy raised an eyebrow.

"This meal looks...normal."

"I promised totally Hawaiian," Nathan said. "Mahi mahi caught fresh. Zucchini and cherry tomatoes grown locally. The peppers are from a garden someone else started right behind this building. And it was all cooked in Big Island olive oil. A 100% native meal."

"You had me worried you'd be serving something off-the-wall."

"Not on your first night. Later I'll introduce you to poi and laulau."

"Laulau?"

"Pork wrapped in taro leaves and baked underground."

"Fantastic," Kathy said. "I haven't caught trichinosis in forever."

She sampled everything on her plate and it was all terrific.

"So," Kathy said. "Give me the history of this place."

Nathan's eyes lit up. "Totally! The first Polynesian settlers likely arrived fifteen-hundred years ago and—"

Kathy held up a hand to cut him off. "Condensed version, please."

"Oh, right. The area around the volcano was in private hands until August 1, 1916, when President Woodrow Wilson signed it into existence as a National Park. It was the eleventh park and the first in a U.S. territory."

Deputy Director Leister had explained to them that the Park Service had been created as a cover story for what was really going on. The government wasn't saving some of these locations just because they were attractive natural wonders. Many were home to the most dangerous species on the planet. The Park Service's secret mission, the one Nathan and Kathy were continuing, was to keep those creatures secret and safely within park boundaries.

"In 1916," Kathy said, "when the only way to get here was by boat, wouldn't this be a pretty tourist-free area to make a National Park?"

"Exactly what I was thinking. Something else odd is that the first people here were military. Sometime around World War I, an infantry unit was stationed here."

"That is bizarre."

"The camp they used is now a vacation spot for military members. I haven't checked it out yet."

"You usually leave no stone unturned in your search for the historical truth. Not badgering the people at the military camp shows incredible restraint on your part."

"Doesn't it? It was killing me to wait until you got here."

"The Deputy Director told us she'd send us where we were needed, though she wouldn't always be able to tell us why up front. If we're here, there must be a reason."

"I'll keep digging through the history for any clues."

"Butler wants me checking the park for invasive species, so that will give me some latitude on scouring the place for any creatures that need to be contained."

"Something smaller than giant crabs would be nice."

Kathy was afraid that something smaller than giant crabs would be unlikely. The Deputy Director only sent them in to solve big problems.

CHAPTER 4

The next morning, Kathy hadn't taken two steps inside headquarters before Butler intercepted her. She was five minutes early for her meeting so his irritation couldn't have been on her account.

"Good, you're here," he said. "I need you to go to this address." He handed her a piece of paper. "Local fire inspector has a dead body on his hands and wants to blame Kilauea."

The address was in a village northeast of the park.

"I didn't think the volcano was active in that area," Kathy said.

"It isn't. You're going to explain that to the inspector. Get going before he decides to give the press first crack at whatever's going on there."

Kathy tapped the address into her phone as she left the building. While the rest of the park had no cell service, the area here and around the ranger quarters were blessed with it. The route came back. While it would not have been far going in a straight line, driving there meant going out of the park, down Highway 11, and skirting the base of the volcano back northwest. A long drive.

Halfway there, she came across a closure of the road she was supposed to take. Her navigation app had not been updated to account for Kilauea's latest activity. A foot-thick hardened flow of black basalt covered a stretch of the road for several hundred feet. This was how Kilauea erupted, not with an explosive bang like Vesuvius, but with a slow-motion ooze. Vented lava would pour across the countryside, burying anything in its way. The slow advance made it predictable, so while property damage was high, loss of life was rare.

This flow was months old and literally stone cold. The government would clear and repair the roads eventually, but this little-used stretch was likely a low priority.

Kathy dropped the Jeep into four-wheel drive low, and crawled up and on top of the flow. The surface was slick and the weight of the vehicle was all that kept the tires from losing traction. A few minutes of slow crawling later, she was off the other side and back on the paved road. She picked up speed and headed for the location Butler had given her.

She didn't need the app to tell her which house she was looking for. Charred ruins rose from the left side of the road up ahead. Smoke still drifted up from remnants of the walls. Kathy pulled up behind a red and white Fire Department SUV. A coroner's van was parked in front of it.

A man in a white, short-sleeved button-down shirt with fire department patches on the shoulders got out of the SUV. His thick, dark hair was parted in the middle and his almond eyes hinted at Asian descent. He pulled out a badge.

"Inspector Scott Saiki," he said.

"Ranger Kathy West." They shook hands.

"I have an arson/homicide and my prime suspect is Pele."

"Pele?"

"The goddess of fire and volcanoes?"

"Sorry, I arrived yesterday and am way behind on the local lore."

"Let me show you what we've got."

He led her down a small incline to the ruins of the house. The ruthless fire had done its work well, leaving mostly ashes. Near the center, two coroner's office employees zipped a charred corpse into a bag.

"He's Sammy Yun," Saiki said. "It's his house and he's the only victim."

"You said this was a homicide. How do you know he didn't fall asleep with a lit candle by his drapes?"

"Because the corpse they just zipped up in there doesn't have a head."

Kathy looked back at the body bag to see if she could tell by the shape if the body had a head. She couldn't.

"Got to admit," Saiki said, "this is my first headless corpse. I've seen plenty of run-of-the-mill corpses at fire scenes, but they've all been in one piece. And to make it even more bizarre, this decapitation had been almost surgical, a clean severing of the head from the rest of the otherwise uninjured body."

"The Fire Goddess is off the hook then, since I doubt she beheads people."

"Cops haven't come up with an answer for that part yet," Saiki said.

"Maybe whoever killed Sammy burned the house down."

"Except there isn't a hint of any accelerants and according to the neighbors the place went up in an instant. I'm sticking with giving Pele credit."

He led Kathy down further into the ruins and pointed out a meter-wide circular hole in the hillside.

"That opening was right under the house, and the other houses didn't catch fire."

Kathy picked her way through the blackened debris to the hole in the ground. She took her flashlight off her belt and played the beam around the inside. It stretched out beyond the beam's range. The inside of the passage was relatively smooth, with only ripples along the surface.

"This is a lava tube," Kathy said.

"So your volcano *did* burn down the house."

"No." She scraped a bit of blue-green algae off the surface. "You get a tube when slow flowing lava cools at the surface while the hot lava underneath keeps flowing. When the eruption ends, the hot lava drains out and leaves a tube. If lava had come out of this tube yesterday, there would be a fresh layer of basalt that might even still be hot. Nothing's come out of this tube for decades, at least."

"Then I have a problem," Saiki said. "Because someone's figured out a way to light an entire house on fire instantly without any accelerant. And that means we're about to have an arson spree."

He looked down the tube.

"The arsonist may have used the tube to make his escape."

"Not likely," Kathy said. "The dried lava inside is usually rough enough to badly cut you, and the tunnels frequently dead end or narrow to next to nothing."

She stepped further in and shined her flashlight down the tunnel. It lit up a jumble of rocks that blocked the tube.

"That blockage settles it," she said. "Neither man nor lava's been down this tube lately."

"Not blaming Pele makes my job a lot harder. Thanks for nothing."

Kathy stepped out of the tube. "Anytime."

The inspector followed the coroner's gurney up the slope to the van. Kathy took the opportunity to give the tube a better inspection.

Large chunks of basalt lay around the tube's opening. The edges of the tube's mouth were sharp and glossy, not weathered. She picked up one of the rocks. It fit into the edge of the tube. One beside it fit on top of that. This tube had been sealed until recently, and from the way the rocks were scattered, it looked like it had been blown out from the inside. Perhaps a buildup of gasses underground had blown it out. But the amount of pressure would have been enormous. And it still wouldn't have torched the building.

She stepped a few feet into the tube. The lower third had deep, fresh scratches in the basalt. On a softer surface she'd swear they were claw marks. But no claws could gouge solid rock. She went deeper into the tube to get a closer look at the rocks that blocked the passage. The rocks had fresh, sharp breaks, and none of the algae-like substance around the opening of the tunnel. It was clear that this cave-in was new.

She and Nathan had been assigned here because something dangerous was about to be set free. She wondered if this might be a sign of it.

CHAPTER 5

Nathan parked in front of the main building for Kilauea Military Camp. Located in the center of the compound near a flagpole and parade ground, the building couldn't deny the military DNA that was in its genes. The office's historic, rustic exterior enchanted him. These were the kind of places he loved to visit; locations that had been maintained with a minimum of modernization. Maybe an electrical upgrade here, an air conditioner there, but the structure and décor of a building, what he considered its soul, remained unchanged. Walking into these places was like passing through a time tunnel, a historian's dream come true. He entered through the main doors.

Once through, he stopped dead in his tracks. From the look of things, the interior had been frozen about 1943. Wood paneling, parquet floors, period furniture in the lobby around a handmade stone fireplace. Vintage black and white photographs covered the walls. He lost complete focus on his investigative mission as the pictures drew him in.

These were military photographs. Soldiers in camp at the site's opening, living out of tents, falling-in for communal meals. The uniforms were vintage World War I, the troops far leaner than Americans today. For soldiers here on R&R, they did not look like they were doing much relaxing. Different time periods had different standards, he guessed.

Other pictures were from later, he surmised World War II from the clothing. One was of people chatting at the canteen bar, others were of soldiers out and about in a much-upgraded compound, including the current main building and some of the cottages around the camp.

Against the wall on the right, two mannequins stood within a glass case. They wore the wide-brimmed helmets, riding pants, and tall boots of World War I cavalrymen. Ration books, small artifacts, and propaganda posters completed the tribute to those who fought in The Great War.

Nathan could have spent an hour just picking through the details in the photographs on the walls. But he was here for a reason. He headed over to the check-in desk. Behind the desk stood a young female clerk with long brown hair. She wore a Hawaiian shirt and looked like she was fresh out of high school. She gave his NPS uniform a once over.

"Aloha, how can I help you?" she said with a smile.

"Is the manager here?" Nathan asked.

The clerk pointed to a side door. "She's out back."

Nathan went outside to the rear of the building. A woman in a sharp, black business suit knelt by the base of the building. Glossy dark hair ran down past her shoulders and splendidly sculpted high cheekbones. She stared at a section of the building where the siding had been removed. A tangle of wires hung out of the wall. She turned to Nathan with a look of anticipation that drooped into disappointment.

"That doesn't look good," Nathan said.

"No, and I'd hoped that you were the electrician arriving to fix it." She stood and extended her hand. "I'm Maize Fukumoto, the manager."

"I'm Nathan Toland. I love this place you run here. Standing here feels like I time travelled."

"All that authenticity has a price. Old things break a lot. And when they do, it's always a repair nightmare trying to unravel eighty years of half-assed fixes."

"That awesome past was what I wanted to talk to you about. I deliver a lot of the history presentations in the park. I was wondering if you had any archives I could study to get a little more detail about the KMC?"

"Do you do a lot of historical research?"

"Absolutely. It's totally my passion. Your doughboy cavalry display is outstanding."

"We have a collection of uniforms we rotate through when we have the time to swap them out. Now, we have some historical records, but be prepared to work for your answers. They aren't organized."

"No problem. I think digging around is part of the fun."

"Then you're going to be in heaven."

She motioned for him to follow and then led him across the street.

"Before I took over a few years back," she said, "we had a renovation. The records had been stored in the main building, but got moved when the meeting room was expanded. They've been over here ever since."

"Correct me if I'm wrong, but there's no active military presence here anymore."

"No, the site is run by a civilian company but we exclusively serve active and retired military."

She led him across the road to the recreation building. They stepped inside to a large room filled with overstuffed lounge furniture, pool tables, and ping pong. A sign on the wall pointed to the bowling alley and canteen down the hallway.

"When the clientele had been exclusively single soldiers on short leaves," Maize said, "this building was the center of activity, with all of this ready to entertain the troops. Changing times and tastes have made the building more of a backwater now. People are here to experience the outdoors and hike the park."

She led Nathan over to a double door in the hallway. A combination lock closed a hasp across the doors. Maize spun the dials and popped the lock. She opened the doors to reveal a medium sized room filled with a collection of mismatched boxes.

"Behold the archives," Maize said.

Part of Nathan was crestfallen at the chaotic, ill-maintained nature of these historical records. The rest of him was elated that so many original documents were there at all. An Army uniform poked out of a box halfway back.

"These are all records?"

"And some military memorabilia. There are a bunch of uniforms that used to be part of a display in the lobby. But the rest of it is all KMC records. In no particular order."

"Looks like my work is cut out for me," he said.

"The good news is, we serve a healthy, inexpensive lunch in the canteen."

"Mind if I take some of this into the rec room to check it out?"

Maize laughed. "I think you'll find some open space."

She left Nathan in the storage room. He unfolded the top off one of the closer boxes. Dust billowed into the air and made Nathan cough. He pulled some yellowed papers from within. The heading was from the Department of the Army. The date was December 8, 1941, one day after the Japanese attack that drew America into World War II. A euphoric chill ran up his spine. Someone held this paper in his hand while smoke still rose from the sunken hulks in Pearl Harbor.

"Awesome," he whispered.

***

Kathy parked outside the KMC Rec Center. It was after nine PM. When Nathan hadn't shown up to reconnect that night, she'd called him and he told her he was still researching at the Rec Center. It didn't take any imagination to guess that historical research had completely consumed her Ranger partner.

She walked into the empty Rec Center to see Nathan leaning over a pool table. Stacks of paper, open ledgers, and piles of faded manila envelopes covered the table. She stepped up beside him.

"Quick game of eight-ball?" she said.

"Sorry, I like, totally lost track of time," he said. "This stuff is a treasure trove, and it's just lying around in boxes. I got to sorting, then reading, and all of a sudden you called and I realized it was dark outside."

"I hope that you found something pertinent, and haven't just been indulging yourself."

"I didn't find any mention of something bizarre going on here. But there are certainly enough holes in the story to confirm that something was going on at one point."

"Lay it on me."

"Okay. First off, this area was purchased by local businessmen at the turn of the 20th century. The plan was to have visitors stay in a hotel on the caldera's crown and see the volcano in action from a distance. The story is that they overestimated visitors and underestimated costs, and then had the Army buy them out to make it a recreation area for soldiers."

"And you don't like that story?"

"It doesn't make sense on several levels. The place has never been at a loss for local tourists. The flat location is perfect for easy construction, with most of the materials available right here at the time. Then add in that, on an island with miles of unspoiled beaches, why would the military, with almost no troops in Hawaii to start with, decide that the edge of a volcano was a place to relax?"

"Deputy Director Leister told us that many of the National Parks were created to secretly put buffers between something dangerous and the public at large. When was this incorporated as a park?"

"The same year that the Army moved in."

"That's a neat coincidence."

"Next historical oddity," Nathan said. "The first soldiers that deployed here to 'build' KMC were sixty-eight infantrymen of Company A, Second Infantry. Infantry. Not Corps of Engineers or Transportation or Signal Corps or another specialty better suited to building things. This was a combat unit. The country was ramping up to send two million soldiers to Europe to fight the Germans. These soldiers should have been readying themselves for war, not building a campsite."

"That does seem strange."

Nathan spread out a bunch of pictures from the camp's early days. He pointed to a picture of soldiers hanging around outside heavy canvas tents at KMC.

"So, these are our soldiers supposedly relaxing at KMC. Living in tents worse than the barracks they'd have left behind. Up here in colder, damper weather with limited everything. And look in the background here."

Behind the tent was the fuzzy outline of what looked like a meter-and-a-half high teepee stripped of its cover.

"What's that?" Kathy said.

"Those are stacked rifles. Who the hell goes on vacation with a service rifle? And why would the contingent of soldiers here need to keep weapons handy if they are building cottages?"

"It wasn't because they were afraid of being attacked by wild animals," Kathy said. "This island has no predators worth worrying about."

"Apparently they thought there was *something* to worry about." He pulled over a map of the park around the caldera. "And look at where the camp is positioned. In a direct line between where the lava pool was at the time, and the road that heads downhill to Hilo, and right at the edge of a steep cliff."

"A perfect defensive position."

"In more ways than one. The first cottages were all made of stone instead of simpler wooden frames. The row of them could double as pill boxes."

"So everything seems to point to the military occupying part of this new National Park to defend the island against something in that crater."

"Especially considering, with the manpower shortages caused by the meat grinder of World War I, these soldiers still stayed put. And I found this."

He handed Kathy a piece of paper with Department of the Army letterhead, dated December 8, 1941. It was signed by the Secretary of the Army.

"That note specifically commands that the military unit at KMC stay in position, and it comes directly from the Secretary of the Army. That jumps over about a dozen rungs of the Army chain of command. Even the besieged troops in Bataan didn't get orders directly from the Secretary of the Army that day."

"Wasn't this written the day after the Pearl Harbor attack?"

"Exactly. The military is awakening to an enormous threat, gathering all forces to defend the islands from a possible Japanese invasion. Except for the soldiers at KMC. Whatever they were here to do was more important than defeating Japan."

Kathy looked across the room at a picture of soldiers relaxing in the same place where she now stood. Posters encouraging the purchase of War Bonds hung on the wall behind the men.

"But all these pictures are of soldiers relaxing here during World War II," Kathy said.

Nathan opened a big ledger book and turned it to face Kathy. It was the sign in book for KMC for 1942.

"And the camp was always full. No matter what was happening in the Pacific theater. And the rules for attending included that every soldier here on leave had to bring their issued service weapon with them. The one that was usually locked in an arms room while a unit was in barracks in Hawaii."

"And they came armed because...?"

"I think that these people on 'vacation' were an unwitting reserve force in case whatever the KMC soldiers were defending against decided to stick its head over the edge of the caldera."

"Whatever it was, or they thought it was, it hasn't been back in over a hundred years."

"That we know of. The military may have covered things up. I need to keep checking. Plus, I haven't dug into local mythology yet. We know that local lore sometimes has way more truth in it than you'd expect."

A dark-haired woman in a business suit stepped in from outside. "The night auditor told me you were still here," she said to Nathan. "We need to lock this place up for the evening."

"Totally sorry," Nathan said. "Got completely carried away. Maize Fukumoto, this is Kathy West, another new ranger here."

Maize stepped over and they shook hands. "Aloha. Are you a historian, also?"

"No, I'm much more the naturalist."

"Then you will love our island. Beautiful nature is around every corner. Even the old lava flows, with no life, have a stark beauty."

Nathan began sorting papers back into boxes. "I'll put all this back where I found it. I barely made a dent in it though, so I'd like to come back."

"Anytime. Let the night auditor at the desk know when you're done so she can lock up behind you."

Maize left the building.

"How much of what you discovered does she know?" Kathy said.

"I didn't tell her anything. And she showed no interest in any of the records, or even in keeping them properly preserved. As you can tell from her instant response with a Hawaii sales pitch, I think her main interest is in running a hotel."

"That's good. The last thing we need is panicked park guests."

"At least until we're sure what they should panic about."

CHAPTER 6

Kathy couldn't have asked for a better assignment the next morning. As the sun rose over the treetops, she was on her way through the forest in search of alien invaders.

Ecologically, islands were fascinating. Darwin hadn't done his groundbreaking research on islands by accident. Isolation meant that species could evolve by adapting to the specific needs of that particular environment. As a result, islands could harbor unique species. The continent of Australia was an excellent example. Kangaroos, wombats, and platypuses existed nowhere else.

The downside was that if an aggressive species from elsewhere was introduced into that island environment, the results could be devastating. An island without snakes can harbor birds that nest on the ground. Introduce snakes, and the birds are slaughtered. Hawaii's biggest mammal problem was feral pigs. Escaped from domestic stock, they had huge litters more than once per year and destroyed the land as they rooted for food. They had no natural predators.

The plant world seemed passive, but the same thing could happen. Aggressive plants could quickly out-compete native species for sunlight, nutrients, and space. Kudzu in the American Southeast was a perfect example.

Hawaii being a natural crossroads, every visitor was a potential delivery system, accidentally or on purpose, for plants that could change the ecosystem. Kathy was on the prowl to find these invaders. She'd kill what she could, mark what she couldn't. Teams of local volunteers were happy to hike in and strip out the larger groups of invaders.

Kathy had parked the Park Service truck at the old trailhead. She carried a backpack empty save for a water bottle. She'd use it to pack out anything that didn't belong here.

The narrow, legally closed trail she walked went through some great flora. The tropical forests here regenerated quickly, a byproduct of a lot of water and sunlight, and a biological adaptation to the catastrophic ravages of Kilauea's eruptions. The areas that natives had harvested decades ago now looked like virgin forest.

Initially, the going through the forest had been relatively easy, the trail untended but still simple to follow. Being closed apparently didn't keep enthusiastic hikers from giving it a try. Kathy's route took her along the volcano's southwest side, skirting the border with the more recently added Kahoka Ranch.

She was especially on the lookout for kahili ginger. The plant had broad, wide leaves and grew quite tall, with a crown of golden flowers this time of year. Very pretty, but it smothered native species.

Forty minutes into her trek, about the time casual hikers would decide to head back for lunch, the plants began to close in and the trail became less discernable. Kathy resorted to a map, a compass, and a little guesswork to stay on the trail. Now and then she had to draw the machete at her hip to cut away some of the faster-growing palm branches that threatened to forever reclaim the narrow path.

The good news was, she found little but indigenous plant life along the trail. She'd come across a few Himalayan blackberries, dug them out down to the roots, and shoved them in her backpack. These unspoiled parts of the park always reinforced her belief that the Park Service was making progress in saving these places for future generations.

Further down the trail, she spotted some kahili ginger advertising its budding golden flowers a hundred feet off the trail. To Kathy, those flowers were a ticking time bomb. When the fruit matured, its seeds would spread more trespassers across the forest floor. That thing had to go. She drew her machete and cut her way to the offender, her eyes never leaving the plant.

She tripped against a large stone obscured by low plants and it almost sent her to the ground. The volcanic rock had been hand-carved into a rectangle. She righted herself and looked around for others. Something poked up from the undergrowth off to her right.

Kathy walked over to find a waist-high wall of hand-cut gray bricks that encircled an area the size of a small house. A single opening in one side looked like it had once served as a door. She stepped through it and inside. The wall was in surprisingly good shape for its age, with hardly a block missing despite a complete lack of mortar between any of them. The site seemed undisturbed. Most park visitors did not venture more than a hundred yards from a parking area. Sad for their experience, but great for this archeological site. An unmarked location on a poorly maintained trail seemed to have made the place as good as hidden.

Kathy immediately thought of Nathan. The historian would be all over whatever this building in the middle of nowhere had been used for. She knelt down to take a closer look at the base of the wall.

Outside the enclosure, something crashed in the forest.

Kathy jumped to her feet and spun to face the noise.

A wall of vegetation a few dozen meters away vibrated back and forth. Then it went still.

Wild hog was her first thought. Impulsive and territorial. She'd seen pictures from the rural American South of eight-hundred-pound monsters brought down by hunters. But there were no reports of them growing anywhere near that large in the island environment. But one would still be dangerous at an eighth that size. She drew her service pistol from her holster.

Then a worse thought occurred. *Poachers*. Possibly for animals, but more likely for plants. Some native Hawaiian species commanded top dollar in the black market. She knelt behind the wall with her pistol aimed across it.

More branches crunched somewhere to her left. This time the noise came accompanied by footfalls. Heavy thuds against the earth, like a rhino or an elephant made. Whatever was out there wasn't a poacher, or a pig.

A roar came from the forest, a loud shrieking cry of fury. More palm branches crunched, even closer this time. Kathy looked for a way out. The rectangular wall had only one doorway. She'd make a lot of noise running through the forest and if this thing was a predator, it might hunt her on instinct. She ducked down and huddled up closer to keep the wall between her and whatever was out there.

Overhead, one of the larger trees swayed, accompanied by what sounded like leather scraping across tree bark. Footfalls crushed the earth on the other side of the wall. A scent filled the air, a combination of sulphur, burnt wood, and an unpleasant musky stench. This wasn't any creature that belonged in the park.

The footsteps stopped. The creature on the other side of the wall huffed and snorted, as if trying to pick up a certain scent, one that Kathy was afraid was hers. Her heart raced and sweat broke out on her forehead.

The animal scraped against the wall opposite Kathy. The stones vibrated and pressed harder against her side. The creature exhaled deeply and the smell of sulphur grew stronger.

The creature worked its way down to the gap in the wall. If whatever it was poked its head inside, there was no way it wouldn't see Kathy. She trained her pistol at the opening. Her pulse beat so hard that the pistol's sights bobbed a bit to its beat.

The creature paused. Its body blocked the doorway and the shadow of the wall now ran complete along its full length. But the creature didn't peer inside. Instead it continued on in the same plodding way. Light returned in the doorway. As the creature moved forward, a long reptilian tail two feet wide whipped into the opening. The skin had a gray, leathery texture and a row of small triangular plates stuck up along the center. The tail swept back out of the doorway. The creature moved off and the sound of it breaking through the undergrowth retreated.

Kathy's heart slowed back to normal. She wiped the sweat off her brow. After a minute or two of silence, she raised her head above the wall. The forest was still. Other than a few broken branches, there wasn't a lot to mark the trail the creature had used getting to or from the ruins.

Kathy stood up and stepped through the doorway. On the ground before her, the creature had left some tracks, giant three-toed impressions twice the width of Kathy's hand. This thing had been huge. And she didn't like the look of the footprint.

She was no paleontologist, but to her they sure looked like dinosaur tracks.

CHAPTER 7

That night, Kathy waited for Nathan in her quarters. He had a night presentation at the Jaggar Museum, and then he'd be over. She hadn't dared try to explain what she'd experienced over the phone, so all he knew was that she was going to share something important.

But first she needed to do some more research in her own area of expertise. What kind of creature had that tail belonged to? It wasn't anything native to Hawaii, at least not during the last several million years.

Kathy went to her computer and called up a website of Pacific Island reptiles. She swiped through several that were not close to what she'd seen. She stopped at the Komodo dragon. It had the same pebbly skin, the same round tail. The one she'd seen had a row of small plates sticking up along its spine, but the rest of the tail was dead on.

The dragon had a long, narrow skull and a relatively wide torso, with four powerful legs that spread away from the body, keeping the animal low to the ground. Sharp teeth designed to shear meat into chunks filled its mouth. In its home range, it was the apex predator.

This species might be what she'd seen, except for the size. The largest Komodo dragon measured in at ten feet. The tail that whipped into the ruins had been that long all by itself.

A knock sounded on her door. She got up and let Nathan in.

"So, you have big news?" he said.

"Literally." She closed the door and decided to lead with what Nathan would think was the good news. "I was scouting for invasive species on the crater's western edge, not quite to Kahoka Ranch. Found something you might be interested in."

She described the ruins. Nathan's eyes lit up.

"Nothing like that is on the park maps," he said. "And that kind of construction pre-dates the 20th century. That would be an awesome find."

"I also think I saw one of these."

She turned the computer screen to face Nathan. The enthusiasm in his face drained away.

"Komodo dragon?"

"Or something a lot like it."

Nathan scrolled down the screen. "Whoa! They grow ten feet long! Was the one you saw that big?"

"I only saw a tail, but I think it was twice that size."

"Sweet." His tone dripped with dread.

"That would be exactly the kind of creature the founders of the National Park System would want to protect people from."

Nathan sighed and looked closer at the dragon picture. "Too much to ask that you'll tell me that the dude eats plants, right."

"Carnivorous. An excellent hunter with keen eyesight and a superb sense of smell."

"If you are trying to make me feel more at ease, you're totally failing."

"If the Deputy Director thought creatures like this were getting loose, she'd send us here to stop them."

"Maybe our assignments could be a little more specific. Give us the opportunity to turn down the ones where we are supposed to face down twenty-foot things with 'dragon' in the name."

"She told us our assignments would have to be vague so that nothing could ever be traced down by the press or any creative conspiracy theorist." The Deputy Director had also alluded to the fact that even her information was often imperfect and incomplete.

"Still," Nathan said, "I'd kind of hoped that after Fort Jefferson, giant creatures would be the exception, not the rule."

"We need to check it out tomorrow. I'm still scheduled to look for invasive species out there."

"I have interpretive talks in the afternoon."

"Then I'll be taking you first thing in the morning, using the excuse of orienting you to the native vegetation." She looked at his hip. "Don't tell me you still haven't gotten firearms qualification."

"Like I've had time. I went straight from Fort Jefferson to here."

"Might want to make that a priority in our line of work."

"I don't know. Isn't dragon slaying more traditionally done with a sword?"

CHAPTER 8

At this hour and altitude, Hawaii was surprisingly cold. Visitors were often unprepared for the chill of a night visit to see Kilauea's glowing caldera. Kathy and Nathan had worn light jackets to counter the morning chill, but the risen sun and the exertion of the hike had Kathy on the verge of shedding hers.

Since Kathy had cleared the trail, they made much better time to the ruins than she had the day before. Nathan had strapped on a machete as his personal insurance policy. His eyes darted all around the forest the entire time, on high alert for giant dragons.

"It's right up here," Kathy said.

They stepped into the clearer area with the waist-high stone walls of the ruins in the center.

Nathan set eyes on the ruins and his jaw fell open. His hand slipped away from the machete. "Totally awesome."

It was as if Nathan had forgotten a giant Komodo dragon might be stalking the forest. He took out a pad of paper and a pencil, and then began to pace off the inner perimeter of the structure.

"So you know what this place was?" Kathy asked.

"Native Hawaiians processed pulu here."

"Just for practice," Kathy said, "pretend I don't know what pulu is."

"Pulu is the Hawaiian term for part of this plant."

He reached over the wall and gave the coiled head of a large fern a shake. She knew what that was.

"The Hāpu'u fern?" Kathy said.

"Yes. As the whaling industry began to die off in the late 1800s, whaling captains looked for another cargo to fill their holds. The Hāpu'u fern produced this soft clump of fuzz along the curls in the leaves. Islanders knew how to harvest and prepare it in such a way that it was perfect filling for mattresses and pillows."

"So they farmed it?"

"More like just harvested it. It grows naturally in locations like this one. But since this is nowhere near any village, the islanders raised this building among the ferns to do that processing. It's totally mind-blowing to find this place."

Nathan walked along the edge of the walls and pointed at some dark, square holes between the stones.

"There were wooden supports and a thatched roof to shield the workers from sun and rain," he said. "The roof also gave the pulu a place to dry before shipping. Can you imagine what it would have been like here, with a dozen men simultaneously scraping and beating fern heads?"

"So, what happened to this place?"

"I guess it was abandoned when the industry later collapsed. I mean, there's cheaper things to stuff a mattress with than Hawaiian ferns, right?"

Kathy watched Nathan get swept away with his passion. He poked around the leaf litter at the base of the wall. He scraped away a little earth to get a feel for how deep the foundation ran. An inch down, the dirt turned to char.

"That's whacked," he said.

He tried another spot further down the wall. Then one in the middle of the structure. Same thing in each location. He gave the stones a closer inspection and the bottom two layers were darker than the rest, kind of caramelized.

"Cool," he said. "At some point in the past, this place burned. It would take a serious archaeological dig to properly date the blaze. The workers likely dried the pulu over a low fire. Maybe the location wasn't abandoned for economic reasons. Maybe a fire got out of control and sent the whole place up."

He swept away more of the dirt from the spot in the middle. He took out a pocket knife and tried to scrape up some of the char. It didn't move. He checked it closer.

"I'm wrong. This isn't charcoal from burned vegetation. It's blackened, fused sand. Almost like the basalt from a lava flow, but a slightly different color and glassier."

"Takes a hell of a hot fire to turn sand to glass," Kathy said.

"Hotter than you'll get from burning ferns. Maybe the volcano ejected material during an eruption that had landed here and destroyed the building."

"Kilauea isn't that kind of a volcano. She tends to flow, not blow. Maybe fissures opened up and superheated gasses escaped and cooked the place."

"There's way more to this story to be discovered."

Kathy led Nathan to the opening in the center of the front wall. She bent down and swept away some leaf litter blown over the dragon print she'd seen the day before. The loose soil had already begun to refill it.

"This is a footprint the creature left," she said.

"Is that what a Komodo dragon print looks like?"

"Only this one's twice the size."

Nathan knelt down and poked at the footprint. "This is bad."

"As the one who was close enough to smell the animal, I totally agree. If these are related to Komodo dragons, they are aggressive predators with poison glands in their mouths. They'll ravage the human population. We need to backtrack this one and find out where it came from."

"Funny how you can go from 'this thing is dangerous' to 'let's find this thing's home' in just one sentence."

"The footprints aren't lasting long. Soon we might not be able to follow them. Not up for it?"

"No, no," he sighed. "This will be awesome. Totally awesome. Lead on."

Kathy followed the tracks back into the forest. The creature had left a trail of broken palm leaves and branches.

Kathy led them down the trail for about an hour. Both of them had taken off their jackets and hung them in a tree to pick up on the way back. Kathy was certain they were well out of the park's original boundary and into the Kahuku Ranch acquisition.

Nathan wiped sweat from his brow beneath his hat. "Getting warmer quickly."

"We're slowly heading down to a lower elevation. The changing plant species confirm it."

The scent of charred wood drifted in the air. A tinge of sulphur followed. It reminded her of the smell of the burned-out house outside Hilo. Kathy stopped and Nathan bumped into her.

"Smell that?" she said.

"Campfire?"

"Or worse."

The trail dead-ended up ahead at a hole in the hillside about two meters across. Trees grew on either side of the entrance, making it invisible from anywhere but right in front of it. The grass around one side had been trampled down and reptile footprints marked up the sandier spots. Kathy stuck her head inside. The burned smell was much stronger. The inside was pitch black.

"A cave?" Nathan said.

"Or a lava tube. Only one way to find out." Kathy pulled the flashlight from her belt.

"Whoa. We're going to like, wander in?"

"No, I'm going in. You're going to stay out here to warn me if something's coming back home, or to go get help if I'm not back in fifteen minutes. Don't come in and get me, go back and get help. Got it?"

Nathan looked unsure. "Do you want me to remind you about how many people have died exploring lava tubes over the years?"

"Not really."

"That saves that conversation." He checked his phone and set a timer. "Fifteen minutes. That means in seven minutes you turn around."

Kathy set the timer on her phone. "Got it."

She walked into the hole and turned on her flashlight. The opening wasn't natural. The earth had been scraped away cleanly, and recently from the look of it. Sharp gouges marred the lower third, the kind of marks that the claws on a giant Komodo dragon would have made trying to get traction.

She tried to remember if these were the same kind of marks she'd seen under Sammy Yun's burned out home.

She had to duck a bit as she continued forward. The earth stopped at a wall of black stone from a previous lava flow. But there was an irregular hole in the stone and chunks of black rock on the tunnel floor. The other side was a lava tube. Warmer air flowed out of the tube, filled with the same mineral smell of the vents around the park. Most lava tubes were dead ends. This one went somewhere active.

She checked her phone. Five minutes had passed. She considered pressing on, but opted to go back instead. Best Nathan didn't get worried. And she should be better prepared to explore a lava tube, though she wasn't sure what those preparations would be.

She walked back to the daylight that beckoned at the tunnel's end. She clicked off the flashlight.

"Nathan, it's a lava tube down here, all right."

He didn't answer.

"Nathan?"

She got to the tunnel end and stuck her head out into the daylight.

A beefy Hawaiian man in long shorts and a dark green T-shirt stood behind Nathan. He held a machete to the terrified ranger's throat.

CHAPTER 9

The man who held Nathan hostage looked like he meant business. Sunlight glistened off his shaved head. Heavy, decorative tattoos covered his neck and spread down to his wrists on both arms. The machete's sharpened blade practically glowed.

"Hold on," Kathy said as she raised her hands. "Let's stay calm."

"Get out of the cave," the man said.

Kathy stepped out into the sunlight. The man looked her up and down carefully.

"I'm Ranger West," she said. "That's Ranger Toland. We both work at Volcanoes National Park. Everyone here can walk away, no harm, no foul. Let Ranger Toland go and you can disappear into the forest."

The man just stared at her, eyes filled with malevolence.

"Here's another scenario," Kathy said. She pointed to the pistol on her hip. "You hurt Ranger Toland and I drop you before you can take even one step."

The man's face twitched. "What are you doing out here?"

"We're checking for invasive species, came across this hole in the ground, and I went in to check it out."

"You're trespassing into the Kahuku Ranch area."

"Which is a part of my park."

"But it's our part."

The man dropped the blade from Nathan's neck. He released him and stepped back. He still looked pissed off. Nathan moved to Kathy's side.

"Are you okay?" she asked.

"Fine."

"I am Romy Saturo Kang," the Hawaiian man said. "I'm a member of the Alika Brotherhood. We protect Kahuku Ranch."

"That's kind of the Park Service's job."

"Kahuku Ranch is ours to protect, as it was before you took the land you now call your park. I don't take chances on patrol. I didn't recognize Ranger Toland, and rangers know to stay out of Kahuku Ranch. He might have been an imposter. Or he might have been dishonest, leading others out here to steal from the land."

"I could have told you who I was if you had asked instead of sneaking up on me," Nathan said.

"Again, I take no chances."

Kathy could not imagine the NPS farming out caring for over half the park to a civilian group, especially one prepared to use force against visitors.

"How did this Alika Brotherhood get this responsibility?"

"Our ancestors were the guardians of Kilauea. For hundreds of years, we kept the mountain pristine, the ground sacred to Pele. But the *haoles* came, the white people. They built hotels by the crater, sent in soldiers, declared the place a park under *their* protection. We were pushed back, but continued to protect the Kahuku Ranch while the owner had us work there. When the land was purchased by the government, we stayed on as its guardians."

Kathy thought there was no way a park superintendent would agree to that deal. But this was no place for an argument.

"This tunnel leads to a lava tube," Kathy said. "Do you know where the tube goes?"

"All the tubes are dead ends, and very dangerous. Could collapse at any time. We don't go in there. Neither should you."

"Okay, well, we need to head back. Next time you see us here, keep the machete in its sheath, okay?"

"It's safer if you just stay off the Ranch."

Kang moved back into the forest without a sound and soon vanished among the trees. Kathy turned to Nathan and gave his neck a closer look.

"You sure you're okay?" she asked.

"Positive. Just shaken up. The dude was dead silent, suddenly right behind me, machete at my throat. Bizarro thing was, his first question wasn't 'Who are you?' or 'What are you doing here?' He asked 'What did you see?'"

"As if there was something out here he wanted to keep secret," Kathy said. "What did you tell him?"

"Nothing. You popped back up out of the rabbit hole before I could answer. As if I'd tell him we were tracking a dinosaur. I have to say, I don't think he knew you were down in that hole. If you hadn't shown up, I think he would have killed me."

"Let's get out of here. We need to have a talk with the superintendent about this Alika Brotherhood."

***

Kathy and Nathan arrived at the headquarters building to find Superintendent Butler at his desk comparing something on his computer screen to some papers he held in one hand. He twitched his bushy mustache back and forth as he read. He looked up at them.

"West! What did you find on this morning's invasive species walk?" He looked at Nathan. "And what are you doing here?"

"We got assaulted in the park today," Kathy said, "by an islander named Romy Saturo Kang."

"Assaulted?"

"He held a machete to Nathan's neck. I think that qualifies as assault."

"He said he was part of an Alika Brotherhood," Nathan said. "He claimed they protect the Kahuku Ranch addition."

"They do."

"Are you kidding me?" Kathy said. "Some machete-wielding private vigilante group manages part of our park?"

"That agreement was in place before I arrived, and I have no reason to violate it. I don't have the manpower to police the entire park. The Kahuku Ranch section is almost completely unimproved and visitors never go there. The Brotherhood provides free security."

"One of the Brotherhood threatened to behead Nathan."

"I think you're exaggerating."

"As the potential beheadee," Nathan said, "I testify that she's not exaggerating."

"I'll talk to their chief about it, make certain nothing like that happens again. As if I have time in my day to do that." He pointed a finger at Nathan. "And what were you doing out there anyway?"

"I took Ranger Toland with me," Kathy interjected. "He needed to stretch a little out of his historian comfort zone and learn about the wildlife."

"I think I'll be the judge of that," Butler said. "Any further work outside of assigned duties goes through me. Understood?"

Kathy bit back a terse reply. She would have loved to tell this man a few things about running a park, but the less she rocked his boat, the more likely he'd ignore her. And the more he ignored her, the more likely she could solve this dinosaur mystery.

"Everything goes through you," she said instead.

"It's crystal clear," Nathan said.

Kathy turned to get out of the office while the getting was good. Nathan didn't.

"Say, Superintendent," Nathan said.

Kathy stopped and turned back around, wondering what Nathan was about to get into.

"How about I go apologize to the Alika leader?" Nathan said. "I ought to be the one to smooth over any of the dude's ruffled feathers."

"Damn fine idea," Butler said. "My calendar is already filled today, anyway. But only you go." This time he pointed at Kathy. "You strike me as a little hot-headed to do anything diplomatic."

Kathy wanted to jump over the man's desk, put a machete to his throat, and then ask him how diplomatic he felt after experiencing that. Instead she just nodded and backed out to the doorway before the temptation for violence overcame her.

Butler checked something on his computer and then jotted down an address. He handed it to Nathan.

"Kaniela Mizuno is the name of the leader. There's no phone. Not sure that he's much of a fan of technology. He holds court at this address."

"Thanks, Superintendent," Nathan said.

Nathan and Kathy left the building. Kathy exploded like a boiling tea kettle as soon as they were out of earshot.

"Butler's an idiot," she said. "That cavalier approach about the Alika Brotherhood is total crap. Especially after meeting Romy Saturo Kang."

"Well, I'll head over and smooth things over with the Brotherhood. They may be more chilled out than Kang. Plus, I can ask about what myths, or facts, they have about giant dragons on the island."

"I'll go with you."

"Whoa, no way. The Super was specific. You piss him off and suddenly you're doing guided tours in Pearl Harbor National Park and I'm here all alone."

Kathy sighed. "Fine."

Kathy knew he was right. But she considered the park she worked at her home. And Kang wasn't the kind of man she trusted to be in her house.

CHAPTER 10

Romy Saturo Kang looked at the door of Kaniela Mizuno's apartment with a mixture of dread and disgust. A summons to meet the *hanale* or the leader of the Alika Brotherhood was never a good thing. The old man regularly treated the younger members with disdain, and was given to long harangues about culture and the past. Kang had no interest in listening to any of that crap, especially from someone so out of step with the times. He knocked on the door.

Chris Lee opened the door. Chris was a few years younger than Kang, and a dozen pounds less muscular. The kid's bald head and the shark tattoo on his neck might have intimidated tourists on the beach, but Kang wasn't a tourist. Kaniela referred to Chris as his right-hand man. Kang thought of him as an errand boy, rushing around and letting the old man stay fat and lazy.

Kang brushed past Chris.

Kaniela sat in a battered lounge chair. The old black leather was riven with white cracks. The dark apartment wasn't in much better shape. The rest of the furniture dated back to the 1970s with avocado and beige tones. Dust coated the faded tropical landscape pictures on the walls. The place stank of damp decay. Kaniela had once told Kang that he did not believe in air conditioning, as if the fact of its existence still somehow required faith to make it work.

The bloated old man needed a fitness regimen. He filled the chair like a three-hundred pound sack of flour wrapped in a muted Hawaiian shirt. Long gray hair hung to his shoulders and there were permanent bags under his eyes. The crescent moon tattoo on his left temple had grown fuzzy with age.

Kang made a passing attempt at showing respect and stood before Kaniela instead of flopping down on the old couch across from him. The old man cleared his throat with a series of phlegmy coughs.

"My sources at park headquarters say that you were out on the Kahuku Ranch this morning," Kaniela said.

"That's what we do, Hanale," Kang said.

"What we *do not* do is put a machete blade to the throat of a park ranger."

Kang had been afraid word of the confrontation would get back to the hanale. "I didn't know who he was. Real rangers know the Hakuna is our *kuleana*." He hoped injecting the Hawaiian word for responsibility would soften up the old man.

"And you should accept kuleana for doing something so stupid as assaulting a Federal employee. Without my protection, you would be up on charges."

Kang doubted that. The two rangers looked a bit bewildered after the encounter, but not angry. Kang guessed that Kaniela was just trying to inflate the extent of his influence. A not-so-important man trying to be important. Pathetic.

"And what are you doing around the puka of the lava tubes? I have reports that you have been trespassing in them."

"How am I supposed to know if others have trespassed if I don't go in?"

"All the caves are *kapu*," Kaniela said, using the Hawaiian term for sacred sites. "Generations of ancestors were buried in them. You know the rules. We are not to disturb their *mana*."

"You worry about some sacred energy underground, while aboveground men tear the island apart. Who's doing something about that?"

"Watch your mouth!" Kaniela said. "Our collective kuleana to this land and our heritage is the paramount concern. The Park Service can void our verbal agreement to tend the land with a whisper. We do not need a hot-head with a sharp blade giving them an excuse."

Hot head? Kang thought. *I'm the only one with a* clear *head.*

"Maybe it should be the other way around," he said.

"What?"

"This is our land, our heritage. Why aren't they staying here with *our* permission?"

"In the Park Service we have found people who share our value of preserving the land. You would have us fight with an ally because of their skin color?"

"They don't belong here."

"None of us belong here. Even our people traveled here from Polynesia. Over generations, Asians, Americans, we were all drawn here to live together."

"And look at you here, Hanale." The title dripped with derision. Kang gestured to the miserable apartment around him. "Living like King Kamehameha in this magnificent palace."

Kaniela's face screwed up in anger. He pounded the arm of his chair with his fist and raised a cloud of dust. "I have had enough of you. You disrespect me with your words, and the entire Brotherhood with your actions. For the sake of your father's legacy I have tolerated you, but now you have gone too far. Get out of my home and do not come back.

And never set foot on Kahuku Ranch again. You no longer have that privilege."

That was the last straw for Kang. He leaned in, inches from Kaniela's face.

"You are lost, old man. Lost in the past, as dead as fish washed up on the beach. There's a new future coming, and you'll have no part in it."

"Chris, get this man out of my house."

Chris stepped forward, chest puffed with pride at being able to fulfill Kaniela's command. He grabbed Kang's elbow.

Kang moved like lightning. He spun around and drove a fist into Chris' gut. The man doubled over in pain, all the air squeezed from his lungs by the blow.

Kaniela gripped the arms of his chair and struggled to lift his great weight up on two unsteady legs. Kang stepped forward and shoved him back into the chair. He clamped a hand around the old man's neck.

"I'll go where I want," he said. "I'll do what I want. No more taking orders from you."

He squeezed Kaniela's neck until the old man choked. Then he released him, and headed for the door. On the way there, he kicked the kneeling, wheezing Chris over on his side. Chris overturned a coffee table and the houseplant on it hit the floor. The container cracked in two.

Kang grabbed a chair and threw it across the room. It crashed into the wall and destroyed two shelves of Hawaiian art. It landed on a glass table and the top shattered.

Kang yanked open the door, stepped out into the blazing tropical sunshine, and slammed the door shut.

He realized that he should have done this years ago. His father Jarrett knew that old man was weak and worthless. Twelve years ago, Jarrett had tried to do something about it.

Jarrett's plan had been to release a devastating lava flow to inundate all of Hilo. He'd rigged up a natural gas-fueled bomb to crack the dome over the volcano's lava pool. The lava flow would scorch the earth all the way to the ocean, and the release of all that pressure would rock the island with devastating earthquakes. The cost to rebuild would be more than the *haoles* could stomach. The islanders would flourish again.

Little Romy had begged his father to let him go down with him to plant the bomb. But Jarrett refused and made Kang watch from the crater rim.

And from that vantage point, Kang saw the explosion that killed his father.

Something went wrong and the bomb detonated too early. Tons of rock and ash blew out of the caldera in a very un-Kilauea-like eruption.

But not a drop of lava flowed. Jarrett's body was never found. Later at his father's funeral, Kang swore that someday he'd complete his father's goal.

But he came up with a different means. He'd known all about the fire dragons since his father had told him the stories as a boy. Released from their lair in Kilauea, they could dole out a much sweeter revenge.

Once he put the plan in motion, he wondered why he had spent so many years struggling under the oppression of non-natives, sat to the side while they stripped the land and then lived better than he ever could? He should have done all this the day his father died.

He consoled himself with knowing the time for completion was drawing near. The incubation was almost complete. And when it was over, then the fun would begin. Did the residents think that Kilauea's recent eruption was bad? This white man's tropical paradise was going to turn into a blazing hell, and there'd be so many fire dragons crawling across the island that no one would be able to stop them.

As he walked back to his car, he was still furious. But at least now he was smiling.

CHAPTER 11

Nathan double checked the address Butler had given him. It was correct. He still doubted he was in the right place.

He was parked in the lot of a rundown, two-story apartment complex. In places, the paint on the walls had washed away to reveal the concrete blocks beneath. Black algae bloomed from pockmarks in the sidewalk. Kaniela Mizuno, the leader of the Alika Brotherhood, a descendant of the royal Hawaiian bloodline, couldn't possibly reside in this dive. Nathan was an underpaid Park Ranger and he lived better than this.

Apartment 117 bordered a covered breezeway between the units. The wind fluttered light curtains behind the apartment's open windows. It was hard to tell if the lights were on inside.

Nathan had changed into civilian clothes for this meeting and driven his own vehicle. The Alika Brotherhood's role in the park's security was not common knowledge. He didn't want the arrival of a uniformed park ranger to draw attention to the Brotherhood. He doubted that Kaniela would want that either.

Nathan got out of his truck and headed over. As he got close to the door, a man in a tight black T-shirt emerged from the breezeway shadows. He was about Nathan's age, but that was the extent of their similarities. The man had fifty pounds more muscle, a glistening bald head, and a large shark tattoo on his neck. His face displayed a collection of bruises and scrapes that said he'd been on the wrong side of a recent fight. He blocked the door as Nathan approached. His stony look promised that he wasn't going to move.

Nathan tried for an easygoing smile to disarm the man. Instead, the guard's eyes narrowed.

"Hey, dude," Nathan said. His voice came out an octave higher than the casual tone he'd intended. "Is this Kaniela Mizuno's apartment?"

The man just crossed his beefy arms across his large chest.

Nathan pulled out his NPS identification and showed the guard. "I'm, uh, Nathan Toland, from Volcanoes National Park. I was researching park history and wanted to talk with him."

The man looked at Nathan's ID, then at his face. "You're one of the new rangers. You hiked into Kahuku Ranch lands yesterday."

"Yes, but, no hard feelings there. Seriously. Just digging for some history."

"Wait."

The man stepped inside and closed the door. Sweat rolled down Nathan's back as he waited in the sun. The door reopened. The man waved Nathan in with a sharp twist of his head. Nathan went inside. The guard stepped back out and closed the door.

The room was a wreck. To his right, broken glass covered the floor under a damaged table. It looked like several shelves had been torn from the wall. On the left the remains of a potted plant sat inside an open black plastic trash bag. Despite the breeze running through the apartment, it still held a whiff of decay.

An overweight man in a faded Hawaiian shirt sat in a lounge chair in front of Nathan. His long, gray hair was pulled back in a loose ponytail. Dark, puffy circles hung under his eyes. Nathan could not tell if they were from sleep deprivation or long-term stress, but the man definitely looked tired. Bruises ringed his neck. Every breath seemed labored.

"Mr. Mizuno, I'm Nathan Toland from Volcanoes Park."

Nathan was going to extend his hand to shake Kaniela's, but the man did not appear to be in any condition, mental or physical, to stand and return the greeting.

"You are the ranger one of my men threatened? I apologize. That man is no longer in our organization."

"I appreciate the apology. I'm not holding the event against anyone. One big misunderstanding. We weren't aware of the Alika Brotherhood's role at the park. What you do for the Park Service is awesome."

Kaniela nodded and some of the tension seemed to drain from his body.

"While I'm here," Nathan said, "I'm looking for some answers about island oral history, and I thought you might be the best source."

Kaniela's eyes brightened. He sat up a bit straighter, though the effort seemed painful. "Go ahead."

"I was looking for any legends about mythical creatures." Nathan didn't want to just come out and say giant Komodo dragons. "Living close to an active volcano must have spawned a few."

"Those stories aren't ones we share with *haole*. They are quick to dismiss our beliefs."

Nathan thought back to the giant crabs he'd battled at Fort Jefferson. "You'd be surprised at how open I am to the unbelievable."

Kaniela stared at Nathan's necklace. "You wear kukui nuts."

"I teach in the park. I like to think that I'm a bearer of light."

The old man smiled. He picked up one of the canes that leaned against his seat and tapped the chair beside him. Nathan took the hint and sat down there.

"When our people first arrived, we did not pay homage to Pele, the volcano goddess. In retribution, she would send dragons to punish the proud people."

Nathan thought that dragons and dinosaurs were too similar to be a coincidence. "Actual fire-breathing dragons?"

"Great lizards that burn a man alive with their breath and then swallow the corpse with one gulp. The beasts would come down from Kilauea and burn the villages, eat the villagers. Often they just appeared out of thin air near a village."

Like they climbed out of a lava tube, Nathan thought.

"Our nation fought the dragons. But finally, the stubborn people realized that Pele would protect them. So, they made offerings to the great goddess. She brought forth an eruption that filled the Kilauea crater, and drowned the dragons in their nest beneath the mountain. We believe that Pele will keep us free of dragons and from cataclysmic eruptions if we continue to respect her."

"Through sacrifices?"

"And through caring for her mountain. That is the *kuleana*, the responsibility, of the Alika Brotherhood. We have been active since Pele saved us all. My bloodline stretches back to the kings that once ruled the island, and all of us have served her."

Nathan's study of history had revealed that most myths started with a fact. Sometimes a tiny fact eventually blown all out of proportion, but the tales almost always grew from a seed of truth. And there was sure as hell more than a seed of truth to giant lizards prowling the Big Island.

"Thank you," Nathan said as he stood up. "This was awesome. I'll drop it into my history presentations in the park."

"Aloha, my friend."

Nathan went to the door and then stopped. "You said your people fought the dragons. How did they defeat them?"

Kaniela looked incredulous. "Spears and arrows could not penetrate their skin. There was no victory. Everyone who fought a dragon died."

CHAPTER 12

Thurston Lava Tube was a major tourist draw, yet Nathan had never been there.

The odd truth about working at a national park was that rangers focused on specific areas of responsibility and so they didn't get to see it all. After yesterday's lava tube experience at Kahuku Ranch, Nathan decided to explore the easiest one in the park to access.

The tube had been named after the Thurston family. Nathan knew their history well. Asa Thurston had been a big proponent of turning the Kilauea area into a national park. He hosted visits by groups of dignitaries around the start of the 20th century. He personally lobbied then President Woodrow Wilson to sign the park into existence. Nathan bet that something more convincing than a Thurston family luau had changed Woodrow Wilson's mind.

The tube entrance was a short walk from the parking lot. The trail to it wound down through some beautiful vegetation, then leveled out in front of the tube. It looked more like a tunnel, easily large enough that a small car could have driven into it.

An older couple in matching Volcanoes Park tourist T-shirts stood just inside the opening, looking wary. When the man saw Nathan arrive, he walked over to the ranger.

"Hey," he said. "We can't find the switch."

"The switch?"

"For the lights in the tube."

"There aren't any lights."

"But it's so dark," the woman said.

"It's an underground tube," Nathan answered. "You'll need a flashlight."

"Then there should be flashlights here," the man said.

Nathan never ceased to be amazed at how some people did no preparation for a park experience, expecting the park to be standing ready to fulfill their needs.

"I'll pass that request on to the superintendent," Nathan said.

The man's face screwed up as he tried to decide if Nathan was being serious or a smart-ass. Then he and his wife wandered back up the trail.

Branches moved on the downslope behind Nathan. He turned around to see a small woman in a red jumpsuit and rugged leather gloves step out from the trees. She wore a yellow helmet just bigger than a skullcap over a ponytail of blonde hair. She smiled at Nathan and her green eyes sparkled.

"Hey," she said. "You're a new ranger."

"Sort of." He extended his hand. "Nathan Toland."

"Suzi Foster." She pulled off her gloves and they shook hands. "I was down exploring some of the smaller tubes. With all the right permits, of course." She reached into one of her pockets.

"That's okay," Nathan said. "I'm not here to check on you. I'm just visiting the tube."

"You haven't been here before?"

"No, I've only been at the park a few weeks. I decided I'd start exploring with a tame tube."

"This is the tamest," Suzi said. She tapped her little helmet. "You don't even need one of these."

"So the rest aren't like this?"

"No! They are very unpredictable. I've been in hundreds of them. Some start and stop abruptly. They might get huge and then very narrow. Sometimes they are more like caves. That's the fun of exploring a new one. You never know what you'll find."

"So I won't be wowed by this tube?"

She gave the Thurston Tube a dismissive wave. "You don't need to go in there. It's been trampled by tourists for over a hundred years. You need to see a tube in a much more natural state. I'll take you sometime."

"Awesome offer, but I've heard they are kind of dangerous. Razor sharp edges, collapsing without warning, that kind of thing."

"Well, sure. But going with someone experienced makes all the difference." She gave him a playful caress to the shoulder. "I'll keep you safe."

An irresistible smile accompanied her offer. Suddenly, exploring a dangerous underground tunnel seemed like an attractive adventure instead of a date with certain death.

"I may take you up on that."

"You free early tomorrow morning?"

Nathan suppressed a little shiver. Tentatively agreeing in principle was much different from committing to actually crawling through underground burrows. But he'd look pretty wimpy backing out now.

"Uh, yeah, sure," he said.

"Excellent." She pulled a pen and notepad from her pocket. She scribbled a phone number on one sheet, tore if off, and handed it to Nathan. "I'll find a good tube to break you in. Call me tonight and I'll tell you where we're meeting."

She curled Nathan's hand closed around the notepad page. Her hands felt soft and warm. She let go and he wished she hadn't.

"Aloha, ranger," she said as she walked away.

He watched her depart until the looks from a few nearby tourists told him he was borderline leering. He cleared his throat, looked the other way, and made a fuss about straightening his campaign hat.

Between the isolation of his last assignment at Fort Jefferson, and the undercover identity he had to assume here at Volcanoes, he realized he'd been at a loss for some meaningful contact, especially with the opposite sex. There seemed to be a connection here with Suzi. No harm in getting to know Suzi better while he picked up some expertise about the lava tubes under the park. Even Kathy would be okay with that.

He hoped.

CHAPTER 13

In the next morning's dusky dawn light, Nathan's truck seesawed as it crawled up the rutted dirt road. There was no denying the butterflies in his stomach, but Nathan couldn't blame them on the rough ride. He couldn't decide if the root cause was the uncertainty of having latitude and longitude coordinates as a designated meeting place, or anxiety over getting to know cute Suzi better in some very close quarters.

Coordinates were how Suzi had set the meeting place today. And how could he expect anything else. It's not like lava tubes had street addresses. On the drive in he realized he'd forgotten to ask a key question. Were those the coordinates of the tube, or the coordinates of where they'd meet to hike to find the tube? He had interpretations to do midday and he couldn't turn this into an all-day adventure.

Up ahead, a light blue Subaru Outback had pulled off to the side of the sorry excuse for a road. His GPS said it was at the grid coordinates. He pulled in behind it. A bumper sticker on the car read: *I'd Rather Be Left in the Dark.*

As he got out of his car, the hatch of the Outback popped open and Suzi stepped out through the driver's door. Nathan got out and they met at the back of her car.

"You made it," she said. "I was starting to worry, just sending you lat and long coordinates."

"Hey, I'm a National Park Service Ranger. We live and breathe lat/long coordinates."

While that might have been true for a lot of rangers, Nathan wasn't the topographic map type. He regularly confused whether the latitude line was the vertical or horizontal one on a map. But the onset of an underground expedition didn't seem like the right time to confess that he was a geeky historian.

Suzi reached into the back of her car and pulled out a set of coveralls. "We'll start with this. Tube surfaces can be rough. Put these on."

Nathan took the coveralls, then made a fruitless search for some kind of private place to change. Suzi laughed and gave his shoulder a playful tap.

"Put them on *over* your clothes," she said. "It's only our first date."

Nathan felt his face get red. But his heart did a little dance at her characterizing their meet up as a date. He slipped on the coveralls.

She handed Nathan a skullcap helmet like her own. A light was mounted on the front.

"Sometimes it gets a little tight in there," she said. "You'll need this. Keep the light off until we get inside."

Nathan strapped it on. It felt a bit like having his head in a vise. She tossed him a pair of heavy leather gloves and he put those on as well.

"How far away is the opening?" he asked.

"We're already there. Behold the *puka*, as the Hawaiians call it."

She stepped to the nose of her car and moved aside a pile of large, dead palm leaves. They exposed a lava tube opening about three feet high and four feet wide. Nathan caught his breath.

"Trouble?" she said.

"Uh, no. I just kind of had more of a Thurston Tube-sized opening in mind."

"It gets bigger."

Nathan hoped that it got *a lot* bigger.

Suzi dropped down and crawled into the tube. Against his better judgement, Nathan did the same. A few feet into the tube he turned on the helmet light. Most of what he saw were the soles of Suzi's feet up ahead of him. He focused on not losing sight of them.

True to her promise, a dozen yards in, the lava tube opened up. Nathan crawled out into an underground cave. It was tall enough that he could stand back up. The cave area seemed to be at least a thousand square feet.

"Whoa," he said.

"Yeah, pretty cool, huh? People ask me why I go down here, and places like this are why."

"How does this happen?"

"In this spot, the lava pooled for a while, so we end up with a room."

Nathan pointed to the opening to a tube on the other side of the room. "So that tube runs up to Kilauea?"

"That one? No. It dead ends a half mile up. Most do. Sometimes the tubes collapse. Sometimes cooling lava seals them. A number of tubes are miles long, though not always big enough to explore. The fun is when they narrow down, you squeeze through, and it opens up again to a surprise like this room."

Wedging himself through a gap between rocks underground didn't seem "fun" at all to Nathan.

A layer of white covered the walls, marred by blue-green splotches.

"The walls look painted," Nathan said.

"It's gypsum. And the spots are rock eating bacteria."

"Something eats rock?"

"I think no matter what, there's something that eats everything."

Icicles of black rock hung from an overhead fissure in the ceiling. Nathan was tempted to touch one, but they looked incredibly fragile. "Lavacicles?"

"Exactly! Squeezed through cracks by high pressure hot gasses. Stalactites in caves form over centuries, but these form over seconds. But one touch, and they shatter. It's one of the reasons we keep the puka covered. The fewer people we get crawling in here, the better. I have permission from the landowner, but there's really nothing to keep trespassers out."

"This is awesome. Stoked that you gave me the invite."

"You want to see the upper tube?"

"I would, but I have to get back to the park. Raincheck on that one."

Suzi gave his elbow a caress. "Going to take you up on that one. Now that you're an experienced caver, we'll go hit some other tubes. I have beautiful things to show you."

Nathan could practically feel the warmth of her touch, even through the coveralls. He smiled.

"Let's do that."

They crawled back out into the daylight. Nathan shed his coveralls and traded his helmet for his park ranger campaign hat. He handed his caving gear back to Suzi. She looked him up and down.

"Always been a sucker for a man in uniform," she said.

Nathan felt his face flush again. Suzi stepped forward and gave him a little hug.

"Call me when you have some time." Her green eyes danced. "We'll do another cave, hit the beach, whatever. Aloha, Nathan."

She walked away to her car. Nathan had to shake himself out of some kind of state of shock and force himself to get into his truck. Suzi's car made a three-point turn and she waved as she passed him by. He waved back and sighed.

Meeting Suzi might turn out to be the best thing about his assignment to Volcanoes National Park.

***

Suzi checked her rearview mirror. Nathan's pickup truck didn't move and the dust trail her Outback left in its wake eventually obscured it. She tapped the infotainment screen and dialed up a saved number.

"Well?" a man answered.

"He's hooked," she said. "If they go exploring where they shouldn't be, I'll be the one they call. And they won't come back."

CHAPTER 14

Compared to Kilauea's lava plain, the surface of the moon looked lifelike. At least the moon had features: craters, mountains, rocks breaking up the plains of dirt. Slow flowing lava from a Hawaiian volcano crept forward like a puddle of spilled pancake syrup. And when it cooled the surface didn't change much. To Kathy, this barren plain on Kilauea's south slope looked like a big, black expanse of poorly poured asphalt.

Eventually it would return to the island's natural state. The sheet of stone would crack. The cracks would create rocks, the rocks create sand. Weeds would sprout, grasses would follow. Deadfall would fertilize the soil and trees would take root. But not during Kathy's career, or even her lifetime. The full process would take centuries.

Today, Kathy was out searching for signs that that process had started. With the Jeep locked in low four-wheel drive, she crawled it across the dried lava. The brilliant sun heated the stone and her tires made a sticky noise as they rolled across the surface.

A wide crack in the basalt appeared ahead. Kathy stopped the Jeep beside it. She got out for a closer inspection, knelt down, and shined her flashlight into the crack.

A few tiny green weeds poked up from the crevice.

She smiled. The indomitable force of life always won. Wipe it all out with boiling lava, and it still finds a way to bounce back. No matter the niche in the environment, something always evolved to fill it. She took out her notebook to record her observations. Maybe the ranger standing here in a forest a few hundred years from now would wonder what it felt like seeing that first sprig of green in a sea of black.

The superintendent's voice crackled from the radio on her hip. "Ranger West, come in."

She squeezed her mic. "This is West."

"Just got a report of hikers in the restricted area on western Crater Road. You need to go get them out of there."

"I'm on it."

Kathy cursed and jumped back into the truck. To her, it was simple. The rangers closed off dangerous areas in parks for the safety of the public. If visitors stayed out of them, they could have a great time with few worries. But somehow there were always a few idiots who had to think they were above the rules, or harbored some misplaced sense of invulnerability. Those people got into trouble, and then park rangers had to risk their lives to save them. She hoped that she could get these morons out of the danger area before any of them actually were in danger.

She hit the gas and headed back to the road as quickly as the terrain would let her. Once on the asphalt, she gunned it and headed uphill to Kilauea's crater. Sightseeing tourists pulled over to let her pass, as if they could sense she was in a damn hurry.

As she closed on the peak, clouds blocked the sun. The landscape took on a grayish cast and the temperature dropped. All of that amplified her sense of foreboding.

She took the south ridge branch of Crater Road which put Kilauea's smoking caldera up ahead on her right the whole time. Its close proximity to the crater's western edge was what tended to draw the thrill seekers, all looking for a closer view of the boiling magma. What they didn't pay attention to was that the white plume that rose from the magma pool wasn't just steam. It was commonly laced with fatal poisons. A puff of a breeze in the wrong direction, and anyone caught in the plume would die. She needed to intercept those hikers before that lesson was the last one they ever learned.

Nearer the western edge, the vegetation thinned out, trimmed back by those intermittent bouts with Kilauea's toxins. She slowed down and looked at the side of the road. Two sets of fresh footprints crushed the sand along the pavement's edge. She drove a bit faster.

Up ahead, something bright caught her eye. A yellow backpack lay on the ground near a jumble of volcanic boulders. As she got closer, she noticed a brown daypack right beside it. They weren't the kind of packs worn by serious hikers. These were the kind kids used to take books to school.

That was bad. The two inexperienced people who left those packs likely weren't prepared for a normal day hike, and certainly not for the kind of dangers they'd encounter on this edge of the park.

Kathy pulled over by the packs. She got out of the truck and pulled on her windbreaker against the cold breeze running across the caldera's rim. A check of the crater confirmed that the caldera's plume was billowing a benign distance to the north. But there was no guarantee that it would stay there. She pulled a small oxygen tank with a facemask from behind the seat and hooked it to her belt. Better safe than a corpse on the ground.

As she approached the packs, she saw why they were here and the owners were not. Between the boulders, a lava tube yawned open to the sky. Footprints covered the sand in front of the puka. As if walking into a restricted zone wasn't stupid enough, these two day-hiking morons had shed their packs and gone down into the lava tube.

The irregular entrance was about two feet by six feet. A jumble of rocks created a makeshift staircase down. It looked like the ground had collapsed to open up the tube. At the bottom was a narrow opening just wide enough to squeeze through sideways. The sunlight didn't penetrate too far past that. If these idiots had just wandered in there and gotten lost in a maze of lava tubes, it was going to take more than one park ranger to find them and get them out.

Kathy stepped down into the tube and cupped her hands around her mouth. "Hello?"

"Help!" a weak teenaged voice responded.

Kathy's heart kicked into high gear. "Hold on!"

She climbed up and scoured the area around the tube. A collection of round stones the size of lemons caught her eye. She stuffed them in her pockets and climbed back down the lava tube puka. A flick of her flashlight's switch lit the tube's nearby walls. The edges looked rough. She shined her flashlight through the opening but couldn't see very far down. Personal risk and professional duty began a tug of war in her head. She decided to check a bit into the cave, but if the kids were too far in, she was going to have to back out and get help. She turned sideways and slipped through the puka.

"This is Ranger Kathy West," she called down the tunnel. "Sit tight. I'm coming."

"Hurry."

Kathy dropped one of the stones where the tunnel's darkness snuffed the natural light. She continued forward. The tunnel branched.

"Where are you?" she called.

"Over here," came the voice up the left-hand tube.

Kathy dropped two stones at the intersection and turned left. Every yard further into this potential labyrinth made her more uneasy that her Hansel-and-Gretel marking system would get her back out again. But the picture of two lost kids huddled in the tube somewhere kept pushing her forward.

"I hear you," she said. "Stay where you are."

A hundred yards further on, the tubes forked. One opening was larger than the other.

"Hello?"

No one answered. She tried again and got no response. She'd have to guess. Which would the hikers choose? She hoped they'd taken the easier route. She dropped another rock outside the tube, and headed up the larger tunnel. Kathy quickened her pace as much as she could. The last thing she needed was to slip and take a dive along the sharp tube walls.

A soft moan sounded up ahead. She played her flashlight beam to the right.

It lit up the terror-stricken eyes of two shivering teens. Dark haired, with similar long faces and large noses, the two looked like brothers, one a few years older than the other. The boys were a mess. Their torn T-shirts and shorts hadn't been up to the rigors of the lava tube. Dirt caked their faces. Blood glistened from scratches along their arms and hands. They only wore flip flops on their feet, and the tube had made quick work of the cheap foam soles. Blood crusted the boys' feet.

Kathy stepped up next to them and knelt down. "Hey, I'm Kathy. I'm going to get you out of here."

"Thank you," the older brother said. "We didn't know this would be so... we got scared...lost."

The younger brother stared at Kathy without comprehension. He kept one hand clamped to his brother's ankle. Whatever they'd been through in here had him bordering on shock or some kind of breakdown. She needed to get them both out of here.

"You're safe now." She handed the older brother her flashlight. "Hold this."

There was no way the kids were going to walk out of here in those flip flops. Kathy shed her windbreaker. She found a sharp edge on the tube wall and ran the seam of her jacket against it. The material tore like she'd cut it with a knife. She cut off both sleeves and then cut both of those in half. She handed the pieces to the boys and took back her flashlight.

"Bind up your feet over those flip flops. We're going to walk out of here nice and slow. Big steps, up and down. We aren't that far from the entrance."

The older boy began to wrap his feet. Every slow motion he made looked painful. The younger brother just stared at the strip of cloth. Kathy began to bind it around the younger boy's foot. Once the older brother tied off his own feet, he did the younger boy's other foot. They finished and stood up. The younger boy grabbed his older brother's hand with both of his.

"All right," Kathy said. "Now follow me."

Kathy turned and began to retrace her path through the tubes. She panned her light back and forth so the boys could see where they were going. She thought she'd navigated through two turns on the way in, but now she'd started to second guess whether it had been three. The surreal environment in the tubes seemed to turn everything upside down. She spied a dropped stone at the intersection with a wave of relief.

"We didn't know," the older brother said. "No one warned us. There weren't any signs."

"There's a big sign and barricade saying the road is closed," Kathy said.

"No, not that. We saw that. There was like, no warning at this cave."

"Common sense says stay out of caves."

"Yeah, but if we knew what lived in here, we'd never have come in."

Kathy paused and turned to face the boys. "What do you mean what lives in here?"

From deep down in the tube came a screeching roar. The odor of sulphur filled the air.

The older boy's face went white with panic. The little brother whimpered. The older boy pointed down the tube past his quaking brother.

"The dragon!"

CHAPTER 15

"Run!" Kathy shouted.

She shined her light up the tube and took off with the two boys right behind her. A second roar came from down the tube. Louder. Closer.

She got to a junction in the tube and stopped. She played her light up the other passages until she found the stone she'd dropped up the right hand path.

"This way." She headed up the tube, the last turn to freedom if she remembered correctly.

The boys followed on her heels. Yelps of pain interspersed their whimpers of fear. They'd already encountered whatever pursued them now. They didn't want to do that again.

The smell of sulphur grew stronger. Another louder roar echoed from down the tube. A dot of dim light shined at the tunnel's far end. The boys weren't moving fast enough to make it.

Unless she bought them some time.

She pressed her back against the tunnel wall to make room for them. Sharp ripples in the basalt poked through her shirt.

"Run! Now!" she yelled at the boys.

They passed her and dashed for the tunnel's far end. Kathy spun and faced the other way. She drew her pistol and pointed it and her flashlight down the tunnel as she backed out. The flashlight beam petered out against the darkness.

Just beyond the beam's reach. Two huge eyes flared red.

Kathy aimed between them and fired twice. The deafening reports echoed in the tube.

The red eyes shuddered back and forth, and then the animal's furious roars drowned out everything else. The bellowing carried a force and a heat that blew Kathy back on her heels. She fired again.

From near the entrance, the boys cried out in fear.

The flashlight lit up a reptilian head straight out of a painting of Hell.

The dragon's eyes sat up near the top of its head. The long snout hosted a large pair of kidney-shaped nostrils. A low set of plates on the top of its head appeared to run down its back. Its gray, pebbled skin carried numerous horizontal scars. It opened its mouth to reveal a bright red interior and a set of sharp, crocodilian teeth.

Kathy barely processed anything other than she was in danger. She fired again and the round hit the dragon in its open mouth. It roared, reared back, and then coughed out a ball of fire.

The ball hit the ground near Kathy's feet and exploded. Flames splattered across the lower third of the tube, looking like little bits of burning gel. One landed on the toe of her boot. She turned and ran. The dragon gave chase.

Kathy sprinted full-out. No worries about the consequences of falling or of careening into the dangerous sharp sides. If she didn't get out of the tube, a bunch of abrasions would be the least of her problems.

The dragon closed the gap. The heat of its exhaled breath seemed hot enough to set her shirt on fire. She fired an un-aimed shot down the tunnel behind her.

She closed on the puka. The remnants of the jacket sleeves she'd given the boys and their four flip flops lay spread out along the tube floor. Running through the tube had shredded them to pieces. Up ahead, the daylight swallowed the boys' shadows as they dashed up and out of the tube entrance. Then they both screamed.

Kathy dove through the narrow opening and into the sunlight. She scrambled up out of the hole and tripped. She hit the ground and rolled left as a ball of fire squeezed through the puka and sailed over her head. It arced over the crater's edge and disappeared into the caldera.

The dragon wedged its head into the crevice in the puka, but only the tip of its snout made it out. It strained against the rock, trying to push through, but the stone held.

Kathy raised her pistol and fired a round point blank into the dragon's snout. The bullet stuck on the surface of the dragon's pebbly skin, then dropped to the ground without even leaving a mark. The dragon's head withdrew. Another roar rose from within the tunnel, followed by the diminishing sound of the dragon's retreating claws scratching on stone.

Kathy exhaled and lowered her pistol to her side. That had been the biting end of the same creature she'd encountered at the abandoned pulu ruins. She didn't realize how lucky she had been that the creature hadn't tried to barbeque her out in the forest.

She holstered her gun and turned to look for the two boys. They were gone. But they could not have gone far with no shoes on their bleeding feet.

"Boys!" she shouted.

No answer.

She looked around the puka. The packs were still there. The boys weren't by her truck and there wasn't anything else to hide behind nearby.

Except the crater's edge.

Kathy's heart dropped. She ran to the edge and looked over. The drop was over fifty feet, straight down. The two boys lay motionless on the caldera floor. In their dragon-induced panic, they'd run out of the puka and straight over the edge.

The wind shifted. The caldera's steam cloud blew in Kathy's direction. The skin on her arms tingled and the scent of minerals filled the air. She grabbed the mask at her hip and strapped it over her mouth. She cracked the valve on the oxygen and inhaled deeply.

The mask was only going to do so much if this cloud was as toxic as it seemed. Kathy returned to her truck and drove well south of the plume. When she was clear, she pulled down the mask and picked up her radio mic.

"Ranger West to Base."

"This is Base," a voice answered.

"I found the missing hikers. We'll need to send in a recovery team to the crater floor."

CHAPTER 16

The red and white medical evacuation helicopter swooped into Kilauea crater from the south. Well short of the billowing steam plume, it came to a hover about twenty feet off of the crater floor. A coil of rope dropped from either side of the aircraft, unwound and hit the ground. Two paramedics in yellow protective clothing and respirators rappelled down the ropes. They landed on the flat crater floor and unhooked from the helicopter. Then a crewman dropped two red plastic stretcher boards out of the helicopter. The paramedics each picked one up.

The helicopter nosed over and flew off in a tight right-hand turn. The paramedics began the short walk to the crater wall and the two bodies that lay sprawled at its base. The paramedics carried no first aid supplies.

Kathy watched the scene, consumed with sadness. Two kids facing down a fire-breathing dragon panicked. What else would anyone expect them to do? Exploring a cave in a restricted area of the park was a stupid move, but it didn't rate a death sentence. She was relieved that the parents were waiting at the hospital in Hilo instead of standing here with her on the ridge. She wouldn't know what to say to them.

Superintendent Butler stood beside Kathy and watched the paramedics getting to work. "This is a real tragedy."

Kathy just nodded her head.

"We do everything we can to warn people about the dangers in the parks," he said, "and still there are some who have to ignore the warnings."

No one posted any dragon warnings, Kathy thought.

"You didn't see them fall?" Butler continued.

"No." There was no way she was telling Butler about the hidden cave opening or what had happened. "I was driving by looking for them. I heard some screams to my right. I pulled over, ran to the precipice, and saw them on the cavern floor. Then I called it in."

Butler put a hand on her shoulder. "No one could have survived that fall. There wasn't anything you could have done."

Except keep dragons out of the park, she thought.

"No, I guess not," she said.

"I'll meet the family at the hospital. File your report and take the rest of the day off."

Kathy wasn't about to take time off now. "Absolutely. Thanks."

Butler headed back to his truck and passed Nathan who was bounding up to Kathy's side.

"Are you okay?" he asked.

"Yes."

He looked over the edge at the paramedics who were strapping the bodies onto the stretcher boards. "Poor kids."

"It's worse than that." Kathy led him over to the puka. "See that narrow opening to a lava tube at the bottom? The kids went in there, got lost. I went in to find them. We were attacked by a giant lizard."

"Like you saw out at the pulu ruins?"

"And the good news is, it breathes fire."

"Whoa. A giant Komodo dragon, with the emphasis on the dragon. That validates an enlightening talk I had with the head of the Alika Brotherhood. They said there are dragons in the volcano. It looks like they were right."

Kathy pointed to the charred hole in the toe of her boot. "I was lucky that my boot was the only thing that got splattered with what it spat out."

Nathan bent down and looked at her boot. "It nearly burned straight through."

"The kids got out first, ran to the edge and either went over it or it collapsed under them. The only thing that saved me was that the lizard was too big to get through the puka."

Nathan stood up and looked around the crater rim. "These are the only boulders anywhere out here. As if they were put here to keep people outside the puka from getting in."

"Or to keep what was inside from getting out. Then more of the lava tube collapsed."

"There's no question these dragons are what Deputy Director Leister sent us to stop."

"And with a lot of nothing to stop them," Kathy said. "We need to know more about these things before more people die. It definitely looked like a super-sized Komodo dragon. I'm going to head back to the residences and research more details on them. We need to find a weakness."

"I'll dig more into the local history. I'm sure that the military was stationed here to keep these things at bay in the 1900s."

"We'll meet at my place after sunset. We're going to need a damn good plan."

***

Kathy got home, dropped in front of her computer, and began a search on Komodo dragons. Her initial look at the information had been cursory. Now she needed details.

The first image that came up sent a chill up her spine. The animal's narrow head was a dead ringer for the one she'd encountered in the lava tube. And she'd sure as hell seen it close enough to make a positive identification.

There were a few differences. First, the dragon she'd seen (and the scientist in her hated to use the word dragon) had red eyes while the Komodo's were black. Second, the dragon she saw had a ridge of plates running along the center of its head.

The next paragraph didn't make her feel any better. Large, curved, serrated teeth shredded flesh like butcher's knives. The jaws of a Komodo dragon were immensely powerful, and an intramandibular hinge could open the lower jaw unusually wide. Add in an easily expandable stomach and the animal could swallow large prey almost whole. Translate that to Kilauea dragon size, and people could disappear in one bite.

As if the Komodo's size and strength weren't terrifying enough, it also had a venom gland in its mouth. If you were the luckiest prey on Earth and managed to escape the dragon's attack, but its teeth broke your skin, your success would be short-lived. Its venom would soon kill you, and a Komodo was just as happy scavenging a carcass as it was consuming a fresh kill.

Kathy thought that venom production would not be biologically useful for a huge apex predator on a small Hawaiian island. But having that gland evolve to throw fire to clear away forest for better hunting, that was the kind of mutation that would make Darwin proud. And a creature that lived in lava tubes would have a level of natural fire protection, so the flames wouldn't bother it.

Thinking about that reminded her that bullets didn't seem to bother it either, at least not the ones from her pistol. She was going to need to bump up the caliber if she was going to penetrate fire-proof skin.

Now that she had a better idea what she and Nathan were facing, it was time to let Deputy Director Leister know. The only two messages Kathy was to send were that the threat to the park was identified, and that the threat to the park was contained. Anything more than that risked leaving a digital trail someone else might follow.

She opened a new browser window and went to an email account she'd set up under a false identity. A slew of spam messages filled the page.

She started a new message and typed in the email address she'd memorized for Victor Moreno, the code name Leister used for their online messages. In the body of the email she typed in the prearranged code message for the threat being identified.

Our vacation started.

She hit send. She logged out of the account, knowing she would not get a reply, or even a confirmation that the message was received.

These dragons were going to be very dangerous. It was no wonder that the government had stationed soldiers around the crater rim. Kathy's first instinct was to call a brigade of them back in.

But that was the opposite of what she and Nathan had been sent here to do. The National Park Service had been created to contain dangerous creatures in certain areas, and to shield the public from even knowing they existed. She and Nathan were tasked with continuing that mandate. Deploying an armored division into Volcanoes National Park was not going to be an option.

She needed to come up with a plan quickly.

CHAPTER 17

Gary Weddell locked the door to the bar and turned off the switch that illuminated the collection of neon signs in the front window. He shoved the keys in his pocket and untied the apron from around his expansive belly. He ran his fingers through his thin comb over the way he always did when he was tired.

It was 2 AM and The Lifeboat bar was closed. Every night the same thing happened. A few dedicated customers displayed a swelling dread of closing time in inverse proportion to his growing anticipation of it. But at the stroke of two, he always got his way. Now he was just a few hours of hard labor away from going upstairs to bed.

Outside, the streets of downtown Hilo were almost deserted. An evening rain had cleared out all but the diehard drinkers on this Wednesday night. Tourists didn't make it this far from the town center, a fact Gary didn't know when he'd bought out the bar from the previous owner.

Two years ago, Gary had decided to restart his life at age 37. He cashed out everything, quit his call center job in Toledo, and bought a one-way ticket to this tropical paradise. Two days into his new life, he sank everything he had into buying The Lifeboat.

Turns out, he'd miscalculated a few things. First, moving to Hawaii didn't make you lose weight and grow three inches taller. Second, Hilo wasn't a sundrenched tourist hot spot and, in business, location really *was* everything. Third, if you didn't like people much, running a bar didn't make you like them more. His enthusiasm for his new life was at as low a level as his bank balance.

But he'd started a plan to turn things around.

One of his less-savory customers needed a place to store heroin. A boat brought it in at night by the wheelbarrow-full, and he needed a safe place to store it before he cut it up for distribution. Gary was going to provide that space.

Next to the bar was a door to the basement. Initially, Gary had planned to store the extra liquor there, until he realized that meant two extra trips on the stairs for each case. So instead he stored the bottles under the bar, and the basement had sat unused. Until now.

He headed down into the basement and turned on the light. The building had been constructed into a hillside. Three walls were unfinished brick. The fourth was black rock, chiseled away to make the basement's final wall. That rock was Gary's ticket to a steady stream of tax-free income.

He went to the center of the wall and gave it a thump. It responded with a hollow sound. Gary had read that old lava fields like this one often had imbedded tunnels or pockets where gasses had once been trapped. That hollow sound promised that there was one right here. Once he opened up a hole in this wall, he'd have access to a secret, readymade storage area. All he had to do was roll some furniture in front of it, and he'd be ready to offer it up as a heroin hideaway.

He picked up a sledgehammer near his feet and dragged it away from the wall. He still had blisters on his hands and stiffness in the shoulders from trying to smash his way in the night before. The rock wasn't going to go down without a fight. The surface had barely flaked despite the beating he'd given it yesterday. So he'd made an alternate plan for this evening.

He picked up a huge duct-taped bundle from a nearby table. Inside the tape was his shortcut, a stash of illegal Chinese fireworks. The stout little cylinders made a headache-inducing boom when set off individually. He'd been told one had as much power as a quarter stick of dynamite. Assuming that was an exaggeration, he'd taped six of them together and bound the fuses into one. Why break his back swinging a sledgehammer when he could let pyrotechnics do the work for him?

Fifteen minutes of internet research had provided him with all the explosives expertise Gary figured he needed. He'd set off fireworks before. How could this be any different?

He did come across a list of recommendations for increasing the charge's effectiveness. One had been that he needed to put explosives in a hole if he wanted them to blast best. Hell, if Gary could drill a hole in the damn wall, what would he need the explosives for? He'd have to skip that recommendation.

He took the rest of the roll of duct tape from the table and proceeded to tape the explosive charge to the wall with two strips in a big X. He was sure that would do it, but better safe than sorry. He laid one more strip of tape across the middle.

From the other side of the basement, he dragged over an old mattress and leaned it against the wall by the charge. The thing reeked of piss, but that's what you got when you stole one out of an alley. He'd lay it over the charge to deaden the sound of the explosion. He was sure he'd seen someone do that in a movie once.

Gary had taken a guess on how long fusing burned and had given himself enough length to get the hell out of the basement before detonation. He pulled the fuse end free of the tape ball. He took out a lighter and lit the end. It immediately began to sizzle and spark. And burn down fast.

Gary's eyes went wide. He might have trimmed the fuse a bit too short.

He dragged the mattress sideways and leaned it over the pseudo dynamite and its sputtering fuse. Then he bounded back up the stairs. He crossed through the threshold to the bar and closed the door. He leaned his weight against it and sighed.

See, he thought, *piece of cake.*

The makeshift charge exploded. The mattress muffled nothing. The thunderous boom blotted out all other sound.

Then came the shockwave. The basement door blew right off its hinges. The door sailed into the bar, pushing Gary behind it. It sandwiched Gary against the wall. His skull cracked against a picture frame and the room seemed to spin. The door teetered away from the wall, then fell flat. Gary dropped like a stone on top of it.

He wondered if this experiment with explosives might be about to kill him.

CHAPTER 18

A boom sounded at the far end of the lava tube.

Romy Saturo Kang whirled around in the tube. The light on his head illuminated only empty tunnel before it diffused into nothing a hundred feet away. He listened in that direction. Just silence.

That hadn't been the sound of a natural collapse. That had been an explosion. He'd long ago considered the lava tubes under Kilauea his personal kingdom. He didn't need trespassers, and he definitely didn't need trespassers blowing stuff up and raising the curiosity of other trespassers.

Kang held a spear taller than he was. The edges of the spear point glittered like jewelry in the beam of his headlamp. He wore a custom fire-proof suit that included boots, gloves, and a hood that right now hung open down his back. A design of red flames sewn into the chest flowed up across his shoulders and down each arm. Though Pele's divine inspiration fueled his mission to rid the island of all that didn't belong, he wasn't above taking realistic precautions. Lava and the dragons were unpredictable. He'd modified some firefighting gear into this suit. The decorative flames were an addition for the future. When the time came to be seen taking credit for what he'd wrought upon the island, he was going to make an impression.

Kang checked his mental map of the tubes. This one dead-ended in Hilo. It sounded like someone had opened up that dead end.

A different sound came from the other end of the tube. The click of claws on stone. The scrape of rough hide against basalt. One of Pele's children was on the way, no doubt drawn by the explosion's sound, and a rush of new scents if that boom had opened access to the outside world.

Kang turned in the dragon's direction and gripped the spear across his body with both hands. One red eye glowed in the far darkness. Kang's heart rate didn't rise one beat.

Seconds later, the dragon's head pushed into the beam of Kang's headlamp. A scar ran along the side of its snout. Its left eye was just a dark hole.

Kang smiled. This was Akamu, the first of the Kilauea dragons he'd met in combat. Years ago, when exploring a tube like this one, the dragon had come upon him just like this. His ancestors may have trembled before the beasts, but Kang would not. The dragon had spat out a torrent of flame, but Kang held his ground in his fire suit. When the dragon had been confused that the human hadn't been incinerated, Kang pressed his advantage by charging forward. With a spear of his ancestral dragon slayers, he'd slashed the creature across the nose, then followed up with a lightning-fast strike to its eye.

The creature roared so loudly that it sent Kang and his spear tumbling down the tube. Later Kang realized that the creature had likely never experienced pain before.

Kang braced for a counterattack. None came. Whatever place in the dragon hierarchy this animal had, it recognized that Kang was its Alpha male. It then backed away and left Kang owning the tube. The dragon never lost its memory of that encounter.

Now, it paused a few feet from Kang. A red, forked tongue licked the air and no doubt tasted Kang's scent. The dragon lowered its head.

"Good, Akamu," Kang said.

He backed up until he came to a side passage. He ducked in, his eyes never leaving the dragon, his spear ready to make a thrust.

The creature restarted its advance down the tube. It huffed just before it passed him. A stink of sulphur and a kind of dry musk thickened the air. The dragon's side filled the tube as it passed and gave Kang a close-up of its thick, pebbled skin. The body tapered to a tail, and then the dragon was gone.

Kang stepped back out into the tube just in time to see the last of the dragon's tail sweep through his headlamp beam.

He smiled. Someone in Hilo was about to get a surprise.

CHAPTER 19

Lying on the floor of his bar, Gary Waddell's ears rang. Blood dribbled from his mouth. He opened his eyes. A fog of black dust filled the air. It settled to reveal the shattered doorframe to the basement steps. The blast had obliterated cases of liquor under the bar and now a mixture of alcohols ran across the floor. He moaned over how expensive that loss was.

He pulled himself to his feet. His tongue pushed something sharp around in his mouth. He spit half a tooth onto the floor.

All he could hear was a dull roar. He touched a finger to one ear. It felt damp. He pulled it away and found the tip covered with blood.

Gary staggered to the basement steps. The light was out. The bare bulb hadn't survived the explosion. Surprise. He went behind the bar and got his flashlight. Back at the steps, he clicked on the flashlight, and headed down.

The air smelled of gunpowder, sulphur, and burned wood. The heavier dust had settled but the thinner haze still diffused his beam after just a few feet. He worked his way down one step at a time. At the bottom, the beam played across chunks of black stone. He'd blown apart something.

Lava dust prickled the back of his throat. He seemed to remember this stuff being toxic and thought he should have wrapped a rag around his face. He coughed and more blood sprayed from his mouth.

The air began to clear as he worked his way over to where he'd placed the explosives. The blast had reduced the mattress to tufts of foam and bits of twisted springs. The sound deadening idea had worked much better on the big screen.

He got to the basalt wall. Or what had been the wall. Instead, there was a hole, about five feet around.

"Yes!" he shouted, even though he couldn't hear himself.

The resulting inhalation brought on another coughing spasm. When he recovered, he pointed the flashlight into the hole. It seemed deep. His heroin hideout might have room for a lot more. Greed demanded he know just how much more.

He stepped through the hole. The walls were almost smooth. And he hadn't broken through to a room. It was more of a tunnel. This was going to be a major payday. He still couldn't hear a thing, but that would probably clear up. And if not, he was going to be able to afford a lot of hearing aids.

The tunnel was as wide and tall as a hallway, easy for him to move down. He turned left and began to explore his new kingdom. A few yards down, the roof had collapsed and blocked it. More proof he might have gotten away with a smaller charge.

He turned around and went the other way. He passed the hole to his basement and kept going. This branch didn't seem to have an end in sight. He stopped and turned back to the basement. This place looked like a goldmine, and it was going to pay off like one.

Something smelled strange. Kind of skunky. No, sulphury. He hoped it didn't get worse and stink up the bar. Not that there were ever a lot of patrons to run off, but he wouldn't want people rooting around in the basement trying to find the source.

A breeze tickled the back of his neck. Then it ruffled his shirt. He sighed. If this tunnel was open to the world, his whole plan was screwed. He turned around.

A giant lizard exhaled in his face.

Gary froze in panic. Hot urine ran down his leg. The lizard's moist, sulphurous breath practically choked him. Two red eyes locked on Gary from either side of the lizard's thin head. The slit pupils narrowed as they focused.

The adrenaline flooding his pounding arteries took over. Gary bolted for the basement opening. His shirt ruffled backwards as the lizard inhaled. Then just as he was about to jump through the hole, a torrent of yellow flames blew past him.

The surreal nature of the sudden burst of fire was enhanced by the fact that he felt no heat. For a split second he grasped onto the hope that this was all some concussion-induced hallucination.

Then he caught fire.

His shirt and hair went up in flames. The back of his neck flash-broiled. Searing pain covered his body like a coat of paint. He screamed in an unholy pitch.

The torrent abated and he jumped through the opening to the basement. Any rational thought was impossible. The overwhelming pain of the fire engulfing his body commanded that he just run, as if somehow the flames and agony would be left behind.

They were not.

Now he could smell it. The rank stink of burning hair. The gut-churning sweet stench of cooking human flesh. All permeated by the overpowering, sulphurous reek of rotten eggs. He made it to the stairway, collapsed two steps up, and vomited.

The spilled alcohol cocktail on the barroom floor had cascaded down the stairs. As Gary's burning hands landed on a riser, the liquid caught fire. The alcohol erupted in a sheet of flames that roared up and into the bar. Gary's Hawaiian dream began to burn.

But he did not care. Unendurable pain had wiped away all reason, all thought, all understanding. Gary spent the final agonizing minutes of his life completely insane.

***

A dragon's head poked out of the hole in the basement wall. It cocked to the right, taking a second angle to better judge distance to the prey it had just barbequed. Its forked tongue slithered out and back to taste the air. The creature stepped into the basement as if in slow motion, one leg at a time. Its head hung over the burning corpse on the steps. Flames licked at the dragon's skin but the beast did not flinch.

Then its head darted down and the dragon's powerful jaws chomped down on the top half of Gary's body. The moisture in the lizard's mouth snuffed out the flames. It bit that portion free, then with a snap tossed the section up and swallowed it whole. A second bite later, Gary was gone.

The lizard peered up the stairway into the burning bar. It seemed to deliberate for a moment, then it started to climb.

CHAPTER 20

Kathy wasn't happy about driving into Hilo to meet Fire Inspector Saiki at a new fire scene. This didn't need to become a regular habit.

The burned-out bar was called The Lifeboat, just outside the city proper. She slowed down her vehicle as she approached the address.

Unlike the last fire scene, this commercial building had more left of it than the house had. Despite the missing roof, the remains of the four walls still stood. The front door yawned open. The vacant window frames all bore scorch marks from the conflagration that had consumed the interior. The fire inspector's SUV was parked out front, but this time without the accompaniment of the coroner's van. She hoped that meant no one had died in this blaze.

Kathy parked behind the inspector's vehicle. She got out and went to the front door. The smell of burned wood and plastic made her eyes water. Saiki stepped outside.

"Ranger West," Saiki said. "You drew the short straw again."

"The park superintendent must think I have a knack for this kind of thing. Rest assured that I don't."

"I have another fire and another hole in the ground. I don't want to hear how much of a coincidence that is."

Kathy knew already that it wasn't.

Saiki led her through the open front door. The flames had reduced the interior walls to charred stubble. The bar still stood to her left, a testament to the durability of the heavy wood of its construction. Just in front of her, a steel ladder stuck out of a hole in the floor.

"The fire started in the basement," Saiki said. "Down we go."

Kathy followed Saiki down the ladder. A half inch of water covered the basement floor. Charred flakes of wood floated atop a thin, oily sheen. The stairway on the left was mostly burned away. A jagged hole gaped in the basalt far wall. Kathy stepped down into the water.

"The fire started down here," Saiki said, "spread up those wooden stairs, and into the bar. This time there was an accelerant."

"So lava is off the hook and this was arson?"

"Alcohol definitely made the fire spread. There's a trail of residue up the stairs leading to behind the bar. Problem is, there's no source for the flames. You can't just drop a match on the wet steps and create an instant blaze like on some stupid TV show. To get a fire like this going, you'd need a lot of superheated flames." He pointed at the base of the steps. "And the basement floor doesn't even show signs of a fire."

"Strange. Any idea who'd want this place burned down?"

"The owner is top of the list. Local wholesalers say he was having a tough financial time of it. I wouldn't doubt it. This place changes hands every two years as some other sucker tries to make a go of it."

"What's his story?"

"We can't find him. Which is suspicious as hell. I mean, your business burns down and you aren't there as soon as the first fire truck arrives? But if it was started from down here, there was no way out once you lit it except through there."

Saiki pointed at the opening in the wall. Kathy stepped over and turned on her flashlight. Grade A lava tube. And the sulphur scent in the air said something had been going on in there recently. She shined her light to the left and the beam lit up a cave-in that blocked the tube. The other, the end that led in the direction of Kilauea, looked open.

"What did you find down there?" she said.

"I'm not going down there. I investigate above ground fires. I'm sending the police down there."

Whatever was going on was just the kind of thing she and Nathan might be looking for. "Tell you what. We are the kind of experts who know all about lava tubes and their dangers. Why don't I get another ranger down here with me and we'll check it out? Honestly, the police are not equipped for the kind of things they might encounter down there."

"Kind of hoping you'd say that," Saiki said, "because the police probably wouldn't do it anyway."

Kathy did some mental scheduling. "How about we come back tonight?"

"In the dark?"

"It's always dark in the tubes."

"Sounds fine to me. I'll meet you here."

Kathy did not need an audience, or an extra person if they encountered a fire-breathing dragon. "You don't have to. The fewer people down there the better. We'll check it out and let you know if we find anything in the morning."

"Kind of hoping you'd say that as well. Then I'll talk to you in the morning."

Saiki went up the ladder and left Kathy alone in the basement. A drip of water landed on the back of her neck. She shivered. But the water was only half the reason. Heading into a cave that might have a Kilauea dragon at the other end was nothing to look forward to.

CHAPTER 21

"We have a problem," Kathy said to Nathan.

Nathan stood in Kathy's housing unit. She had only unpacked the barest of necessities and cardboard boxes filled most of the living room. Too much was happening too quickly for her to be self-conscious about the chaos.

"I just got back from a second fire, this one in downtown Hilo. Both fires had lava tubes that opened up under the buildings. Both fires looked like arson but there was no evidence of arson. These are not coincidences. Kilauea dragons are getting into town through lava tubes."

"A caver I met told me that even the experts don't know how many lava tubes there are throughout the island," Nathan said. "Some of them are mapped, but plenty more are not, or aren't even discovered."

"That's going to make blocking them all impossible," Kathy said. "So we're going to have to stop the dragons at their nest."

"Nest?"

"If these are like Komodo dragons on steroids, and everything indicates they are, they have a nest somewhere. Komodos live above ground in expropriated nests of large ground birds. I'm going to guess that a Kilauea dragon nest will be underground since that's their environment."

"Whoa. Let's do some pondering. You want to crawl through the lava tubes looking for a nest of fire-breathing dragons?"

"In a nutshell."

"More like just nuts. I've been in those tubes. They aren't safe, even without dragons in them."

"We can't just let the dragons keep attacking the community. The next time the body count of innocent victims might be who knows how high. We need some reconnaissance to see what's going on, then make a plan to put a stop to it."

"This is totally out of our areas of expertise. Those kids on the crater rim got lost in minutes in a set of lava tubes. Let me get my caving expert to come with us."

"I don't know," Kathy said. "The more people who know the truth about what's crawling around under Kilauea, the more likely that truth will get out."

"I won't tell her the truth. We'll just be exploring the tubes to see if they lead into the park. I'll redirect her from anything strange we find."

"Unless we find a dragon."

"We'll deal with that if we have to," Nathan said. "But without an expert, we might get lost or hurt down there, and then there's no one to keep the dragons from escaping Kilauea."

Kathy weighed the risk of widening the circle of the informed. But the next time a dragon emerged in downtown Hilo, that circle would be catastrophically wider.

"Okay," Kathy said. "Let's bring her in, explaining as little as possible."

Nathan smiled. "Sweet. You won't regret it."

Kathy was very afraid that she would.

"I know what gear we'll need to go in," Nathan said. "I'll set us up."

Kathy checked the time on her phone. "Okay. Let's meet with your expert at the puka at 8:30, after dark and after most traffic has died down. I don't know what kind of defense we can have against fire-breathing dragons. We don't have firefighter suits, and they'd be too bulky anyway down in the tubes."

"I think I might have an answer for that as well. I'll meet you there."
***

A half hour later, Nathan entered the KMC Rec Center. Two kids played ping pong in such a way that it seemed they didn't know that the ball was ever supposed to touch the table.

Something smelled awful, as if someone had marinated spoiled meat in sour milk. He followed the smell back to the canteen.

The setup looked like a movie theater food counter, with a few tables in front. The area was dark with the only light coming from a doorway behind the counter. Nathan approached the doorway. The stink got worse with every step. He looked inside.

Maize Fukumoto stood in front of the open stainless-steel door of a walk in cooler. Water had run out of the bottom and made a puddle on the floor. She leaned on a mop and had a furious look on her face.

"Hey there," Nathan said.

Maize looked up and managed if not a smile, at least a lower level of anger. "Nathan, if you were dropping by for a meal, we're closed."

"I can see, and smell, that. What happened?"

"I'm so mad. Upper management retrofitted the cooler with a new refrigeration system. Battery backup compressor, ultra-green refrigerant gasses. All very environmentally friendly." She paused as if she realized how venomously she'd spit out the last few words. "Don't get me wrong. I work in a National Park. I fully support green technology. As long as it works. Obviously this didn't."

"And by the stench I'm guessing that everything in there is spoiled."

"Oh, yes. And out here…" She closed the cooler door to reveal the wall behind it. "…another fun mess to come."

A layer of ice encased the bottom four feet of the wall. Melt water dripped from the bottom edge.

"Looks more like the decorations at the Glacier National Park snack bar," Nathan said.

"The leaking refrigerant sprayed the wall at high pressure. That ice is inches thick. I need to get people to chip that off before it melts and floods the kitchen. The refrigeration company brought out a replacement unit."

Maize pointed across the room. Near the wall stood a metal cylinder three feet high and a foot around. The base was made of a compressor studded with cooling fins. Metal tubes ran along one side.

"But the fittings on that model aren't the same as on the current one. Of course. So they need to order them from the mainland. Of course."

"A downside to island living," Nathan said.

"You stopped by to chip ice for me?" Maize said.

"I wish I could say yes, but I came to do a little more research."

"You know your way to the storage room and the combination to the lock is 1916," she said.

"The year this became a park."

"Easier to remember," Maize said. "I'll be in here mopping if you need me."

Nathan felt awful not helping her with that mess, but he and Kathy had a pressing dragon problem to attend to. He made his way back to the storage room and dialed in the code for the lock. He popped it off, opened the door, and flipped on the light. He gave the boxes of memorabilia a quick once over and discovered the object of his search.

He retrieved a box from the back. It was piled high with uniforms. A sage green sleeve hung over one corner.

He began to unpack the box, pulling out uniforms from different services and different eras. Army, Air Force, Navy, Marines. He laughed as he discovered two bright blue and white reproduction uniforms from the Revolutionary War. He was going to totally volunteer to help manage the lobby's historical exhibits once this dragon mess was straightened out.

Then he saw what he was looking for, the other end of the sage green sleeve. He pulled out two U.S. Army flight suits. The zippered coveralls were made of Nomex, a very flame-resistant material. Not as protective as a firefighter's gear, but way better than a Park Service ranger uniform, and not as bulky as the yellow turnout gear the firefighters wore. Plus, Nathan had access to these. Now he just needed some protection for the parts of them the coverall missed.

He rooted around in the box and pulled out two pairs of matching Nomex gloves. That would get everything covered except their heads. He squeezed between boxes to a mound of helmets and caps in the corner. Two flight helmets poked out of the pile. They would cover the head more completely than a combat helmet and had a visor that slid down over the eyes. He tucked one inside the other and carried them back to the door. On the way out of the room, he scooped up the flight suits and gloves. He closed and locked the door behind him.

They were going to look a bit like they were costumed for Halloween, but if the uniforms ended up saving their lives, then it would be worth feeling like a child playing dress up for a while.

The kids at the ping pong table had departed. Nathan wondered if they'd gotten bored or if they'd lost the ball. The building was empty. He took out his phone and dialed Suzi's number. She answered after a few rings.

"Nathan!"

"Hey, Suzi."

"I was afraid that our lava tube adventure might have scared you off."

"Not at all. Just the opposite, in fact. I was wondering if you were up for exploring a new tube?"

"Like that's even a question? Hell yeah. When and where?"

"Planning on tonight at The Lifeboat bar in Hilo. It burned down and exposed a tube underneath. It looks like it heads back to the park. We realized that it would be last minute, but we wanted a pro with us when we went to check it out."

"We?"

"Ranger Kathy West is coming. We go way back. She's cool."

"Well, I'd rather it was just us, but I'll force myself to deal with company. I'll be there."

"Awesome. See you about 8:30."

He hung up and couldn't help but smile, even though he'd just arranged an expedition to confront fire-breathing dragons. He definitely had two things to do after all this dragon drama was over: Work on the KMC historical displays, and work on getting something started with Suzi.

***

As soon as Nathan hung up, Suzi dialed Kang.

"Hello?"

"It's on. They are going into a new tube under the Lifeboat bar downtown."

"See that they don't come back out."

"Hey, there's two of them and one of me. The doofus isn't ever armed but the other ranger might be. I don't like those odds."

Kang paused. "I'll make sure she doesn't get there. It will just be the two of you and you need to convince him to go in without her."

"Got it."

"And once you're in there, you don't have to kill him if you get squeamish. Just seal him in. Hungry dragons will do the rest."

CHAPTER 22

Kathy paced around her quarters, unable to sit still.

She'd been consumed by worries about what she and Nathan had to do in a few hours. Exploring a lava tube was dangerous. Exploring one that might have a dragon at the other end was *extremely* dangerous.

Plus, the caver that Nathan had recruited was a wild card dealt into their hand. Sure, having some expertise was a big plus. But letting an outsider be part of their secret mission, even without her knowing the details behind it, filled Kathy with dread.

She checked the clock. She didn't need to leave for hours. Knowing that just made the time seem to pass even slower.

She had to admit that she liked the ranger quarters. Built during the Depression Era park building heyday, the little wooden house had been given just the right amount of upgrades with electricity, indoor plumbing, and recently wi-fi, without losing the simple charm of its pre- World War II construction. The wooden paneling and furniture were all vintage, the fireplace hand-made from unfinished lava rock.

She went into the kitchen to get some coffee started. Might as well get caffeinated for the long night ahead.

Lights blazed to life at the front of her cabin and sent shafts of white through the window slats. She jumped and spun around. There weren't any streetlights along the road and her cabin faced a sandy lot filled with scrubby bushes. She stepped over and peered through the slats.

Her Jeep headlights were on.

"What the hell?" she whispered.

She grabbed her keys from the table by the door. Had the doors unlocked remotely and set the lights off? A Jeep-loving friend of hers had once told her she never locked the vinyl doors so that thieves could just steal what they wanted, instead of cutting open the doors and still stealing what they wanted. She'd followed that advice. She hit the remote to lock the doors. That would also turn off the lights.

She heard the car chirp its reply that the doors had locked. But the lights stayed on.

Kathy had nothing against having modern conveniences. But when the technology morphed from helpful to infuriating, it made her long for simpler things, which might have been one of the reasons she liked this little cabin of a house. There was no telling what was wrong with the Jeep. She wondered if this fun little issue was what made the previous owner trade it in.

"On the bright side," she said to herself, "it happened now, instead of when I wouldn't notice it for hours and it would kill the battery."

She went outside and crossed through the headlight beams to the vinyl driver's door. She hit the unlock button on the remote and pulled open the door.

The headlight switch was in the on position.

A chill ran up her spine. Someone had turned on the lights. All her senses went to high alert.

She reached for her sidearm and realized that she hadn't put her gun belt on yet. Then she realized she'd left the door to her quarters open.

"Dammit."

She spun around to get back inside. A human shape blocked the way.

Before she could react, something heavy crashed into the left side of her face. The impact threw her against the Jeep door and she dropped to the ground. Her head reeled. She tried to process the attack, raise a defense, but she couldn't make sense of anything, except that she needed to be safer. She moved to crawl under the Jeep.

A second blow crashed against the back of her head, and the night's darkness became absolute.

CHAPTER 23

Nathan paced at the lava tube entrance by flashlight. Kathy was the kind of person who considered herself late if she wasn't early. Since it was after 8:30 and she wasn't here, she was even late by normal standards. They needed to be up this tube and back before today turned into tomorrow.

The burned-out basement was spooky enough without worrying about Kathy. In the darkness, the ravaged building was about as inviting as a graveyard. The acrid smell of smoke made the air seem heavy. A quarter inch of ashy mud coated the basement floor where the water from the fire department had drained away or evaporated.

Nathan wore the Nomex flight suit and the gloves he'd...well...stolen from KMC. A flight helmet hung from a hook on the wall. A set of the same items waited in his truck for Kathy when she arrived.

He'd parked his personal vehicle several streets over to keep from arousing suspicion. Kathy said that they technically had the permission from the fire department to explore this part of the crime scene, but he still didn't want neighbors dropping by and getting nosy. He realized that he should have told Suzi to do the same thing, but it was a little late to do that now. Plus, implying that this whole escapade was clandestine might scare her off.

He was looking forward to having her here for the technical expertise, and even more so for her company. Caving was a poor substitute for dating, but he had high hopes that it might lead to dinner and a movie at some point.

Nathan took out his phone and dialed Kathy. After a few rings, the call rolled to voicemail. That was as abnormal as her being late. In a situation like this, Kathy would not only have answered her phone, she would have already called to tell Nathan she'd been delayed.

Door hinges moaned upstairs. Nathan froze. The realization that some criminal element might take advantage of the darkness to loot the burned-out bar occurred to him. Nathan killed his flashlight and backed into the opening to the lava tube.

Footsteps made floorboards creak overhead. A shadowy mass appeared where the ladder poked through the hole in the floor. A bright flashlight beam came to life and probed the basement floor. Nathan held his breath.

"Nathan?" Suzi said.

Thank God, Nathan thought. He stepped out of the opening and tried to squeeze the fear from his voice. "Right down here."

Suzi aimed the beam at his face. He shielded his eyes with one hand and waved with the other.

"What are you stumbling around in the dark like that for?" she said.

"Conserving batteries?" He really hadn't intended that to sound like a question.

Suzi descended the ladder to the basement. Nathan played his light in that direction and stepped over to steady the ladder. Suzi had on her caver coveralls and her helmet, though it was unstrapped. She also shouldered a backpack that sagged from the weight inside it. She hopped off the end of the ladder and hit the basement floor with a splat. She wobbled and Nathan put an arm around her shoulder to steady her. She looked up at him and smiled.

"Thanks, hero." Suzi looked around the basement. "Where's the other ranger?"

Nathan checked his watch for the hundredth time. "She should have been here a while ago."

Suzi's face screwed up in confusion as she looked him over more closely. "What are you wearing?"

Nathan tensed up. He was torn between giving her a warning about the potential need for fireproof clothing and keeping the whole idea of underground dragons a secret.

"This was as close to caving clothes as I could find," he said.

She looked at the suit and then the flight helmet on the wall and smiled. "Well, got to say I like it. Very retro *Top Gun*. Go, Maverick."

He relaxed and promised himself to prioritize her safety if they encountered anything in the tube.

Suzi checked her watch. "How long do you want to wait?"

"A bit longer."

Nathan took out his phone and sent Kathy a text asking where she was. He hoped that maybe if her phone didn't have a strong enough signal for a call, it might have enough for a text. Honestly, he didn't even know if phones worked that way, but the hope let him do something.

Suzi took two large handheld lights from her pack and handed one to Nathan. She shined her light around the edge of the puka in the wall, then into the lava tube.

"Ooh, nice tube! Standing headroom. You know how to spoil a girl."

She took out a hand-drawn map of lava tubes and shined her light down on it for the two of them to read.

In the map's center was an outline of the crater of Kilauea. A network of dark lines spread out from the crater in all directions like a kid's drawing of the sun. Each of the lines had notes in specific locations warning of collapses or tight passages. Suzi pointed to an unmarked area near the bottom of the map.

"We are right about here," she said. "This is an undiscovered tube. I guess the fire weakened the wall and it collapsed to expose it."

"Most likely," Nathan said.

Nathan took the map and studied the area around the west side of the crater where the boys had found the hidden puka. There wasn't any notation of it there. Good as the cavers thought the map was, it was obviously quite incomplete.

"Should we get started?" Suzi said.

Nathan checked his phone again. Still no word from Kathy. He imagined her telling him in no uncertain terms to get going without her. He tucked the lava tube map in his pocket.

"Let's get going," he said. "I'll go first."

Suzi smiled. "By all means."

He put on the flight helmet and the two stepped into the tube. A collapse blocked the passage to one side, so Nathan took the other tube. A few feet in, his helmet scraped the ceiling and he had to stoop a bit. The walls were relatively smooth, not anywhere near as jagged as the tube he and Suzi had explored earlier. The idea that they might have been polished by centuries of passing dragon skin gave him a serious shudder.

A hundred yards in, the tunnel hadn't branched yet, which made Nathan much more comfortable that they could find their way back out in a hurry. Kathy had said the kids had gotten lost even though they were close to the puka.

"So," Suzi said, "what is it you're hoping to find down here?"

"Find? Nothing. Just seeing if this tube leads into the park. We'll want to seal it to keep inexperienced people from wandering into it."

Suzi didn't say anything. Nathan hoped she'd just accept his lame answer and not pursue this line of questioning.

They continued through the tube as it narrowed and made a sharp curve. Nathan had to go through the gap sideways. Suzi had to shed her pack to follow. She squeezed through, but her backpack hung up between the rocks as she pulled it through after her. Nathan stepped over and grabbed a strap to give it a yank.

"No!" Suzi said. She pushed him away. "I've got it."

She eased the backpack through the opening after her. A smile replaced the scared look on her face. She patted Nathan's arm.

"Don't want you shredding my stuff being all manly," she said.

Nathan didn't think that would have been a problem.

On the other side of the kink in the tube, the smell of sulphur was much stronger. The air grew noticeably warmer. He took out the map and shined his light on it. Suzi sidled up beside him.

"Where do you think we are?" he said.

She checked a compass on her wrist. "We've been going due east for a while, then that curve turned us southeast." She pointed to a spot on the map with no lava tube marked. "I'd say about here."

The spot was almost inside the park boundaries.

After walking for a few more minutes, Nathan thought he saw lavacicles hanging from the ceiling, the first geologic formation they'd seen in the cave. He kept his flashlight trained on them as he got closer. A few were quite large.

But by the time he stood under them, he could tell they were something much more organic. Tree roots. Water dripped down from the longest one.

"Cool," Suzi said as she caught up with him. "We must be close to the surface here."

"Close enough that it might cave in?"

"Oh, sure. In a few decades. Not while we're down here."

Nathan continued forward while Suzi gave the tree roots a closer inspection. He began to worry again about Kathy. Only something catastrophic would have kept her from exploring this tube. He coughed as the smell of sulphur ramped up a few notches.

"Do we need to worry about being overcome by gasses down here?" he asked Suzi.

She didn't answer.

He stopped and played his flashlight back down the tube. He was alone.

"Suzi!" he called out. His cry echoed off the stone walls.

His imagination ran wild at the multiple tragedies that could have befallen her in the tube. He retraced his steps at a jog, sweeping his flashlight across the floor, and hoping he wouldn't find anything. He passed back under the protruding tree roots. Still nothing. He moved faster.

A few yards farther on, he saw a paper bag tucked into one side of the tube. That hadn't been there before. He knelt down and picked it up. He shined his light inside.

A red cardboard block in the bottom had VENTEX stenciled on it followed by a few lines of gray, government-style identification numbers along one side. A pencil-sized metal tube stuck part of the way out of one side and two wires from the tube ran to a small box. Red numbers on the box were counting down from eleven.

"Holy hell," Nathan whispered. He wasn't an explosives expert, but he'd seen enough documentaries on terrorism to know what a bomb looked like.

Drop it? Throw it? Would it explode if I tried to take it apart? All of these questions flooded into his brain at once.

Before he could answer any of them, an explosion rocked the tunnel ahead of him. A wall of flame and dust swelled out of the darkness, heading straight for Nathan.

***

On the other side of the narrowed passage in the tube, Suzi stood up and brushed some basalt dust from her coveralls. Placing the charge on the other side of the bend in the tunnel had helped shield her from the blast. She turned her flashlight on and checked the tube. The blast had sealed it.

That first blast would send Nathan running back to investigate. The way she'd timed the other charge, he'd be up against the jammed passage when the second block of Ventex detonated behind him. Best case, the whole tube would collapse on him. Worst case, he'd just be sealed inside with no way to get out. Either way, she'd accomplished her mission. And if anyone searched for Nathan and found him, he'd look like another tragic lava tube fatality.

Now, as long as Kang accomplished his mission and got rid of the other ranger, they'd be home free to finish the plan to let the Kilauea dragons retake their home island.

She hurried for the tube exit. No need to await the second blast. With tons of rock sealing the tube, she might not even hear it.

The same way no one would hear Nathan if he survived to cry for help.

CHAPTER 24

Nathan coughed as he dragged himself to his knees. The tube was pitch black and the air was so thick with basalt dust he could barely breathe. Stones and dirt rolled off his back. His helmet felt loose on his head, though the chin strap had stayed secure through the explosion.

He rewound the last few minutes of his life. *Explosion*, not a cave in. A bomb had gone off. He was sure of that because when it had, he'd had another one in his hands.

He ran his fingertips across the rubble on the tube floor in search of the flashlight he'd been holding when the explosion happened. All he felt were bits of rock. Then he touched the flashlight's rectangular plastic cover. He grabbed it and flicked the on switch. Nothing happened. He shook it and it rattled. Destroyed. Just because he'd made it through the explosion didn't mean the flashlight would.

He remembered the smaller light on his belt, retrieved it and turned it on. The tiny beam could barely penetrate the thick, swirling dust. He stood up into clearer air and sent the beam back in the direction of the tunnel exit. The passage was now a mass of rubble. Even if he could move the largest of the stones, which he couldn't, there wasn't any guarantee the rest of the tube wouldn't collapse on top of him doing it.

He took his flight helmet off. It came apart in two pieces. It might not have had to save anyone's life in Vietnam, but it had certainly saved his. He remembered there was a bomb somewhere in the tube ready to give killing him a second try. He dropped the helmet sides on the floor and sent his flashlight beam across the rubble. He spied the shredded paper bag a dozen feet away.

He stepped over to it. With one finger, he opened the bag. The cardboard block of explosives was still in there. The timer and what he guessed had been the detonator were gone, probably ripped out during the explosion. The first near miss detonation had saved him from certain death from the second.

But that had been the plan. Seal the tube with the first charge, kill him with the second charge when he went back to investigate. Terrorists used the same tactic to enhance casualty rates. Then a horrible realization hit him like a punch in the gut.

Suzi had done this. She'd backtracked down the tube, set the charges to kill him, and escaped.

He leaned back against the wall, consumed by a sense of betrayal. How could she do that? She seemed so nice, so genuine. Then he asked himself why she would do it. He didn't know her well enough for it to have been personal, which meant she had to be part of whatever plot was trying to set the Kilauea dragons free from the park. Which meant no one could be trusted. He needed to get out of here and warn Kathy. He carefully put the explosive charge on the ground.

The airborne dust settled. He picked his way through the tube and past the tree roots. With no way to the entrance, he had to hope there was an exit up ahead.

Then from the tube's far end came the sound of something moving against stone. Like the chorused click and scrape of knife blades scuttling across the surface of the tube. The sulphur smell grew stronger.

Nathan backed against the tube wall and stood still. The noise continued, louder. He shined his flashlight down the tube.

The beam lit up two large red eyes in the darkness.

"Oh no."

Then a stream of fire rocketed down the tunnel. The flames bounced off the ceiling and fell short of Nathan, but the heat did not. A shockwave of sulphur-infused hot air rolled over him. It felt like someone had opened a door to Hell.

A thin trail of flames now ran along the tube floor. Into that orange glow poked the head of a Kilauea dragon, looking exactly like a scaled-up version of the pictures he'd seen with Kathy. A red, forked tongue whipped out to taste the air. Its head turned slightly and two red eyes narrowed as it spotted Nathan.

Nathan turned and ran, fully knowing he had nowhere to run to. The blocked end of the tunnel lay just ahead.

The dragon shrieked and its shrill cry echoed off the lava tube walls. Its head bent back and it sent another spurt of flame bouncing off the ceiling and onto the floor just behind Nathan. Heat curled the hairs on the back of his neck.

Nathan ducked as he ran under the protruding tree roots. Right around the next curve he'd hit the rubble wall. From the scratching sounds behind him, the dragon wasn't slowing down.

Then Nathan saw the paper bag on the floor with the explosives inside. He had a very bad, very desperate idea.

He grabbed the bag and shoved it into the tangle of roots in the ceiling. Then he backed up to just short of the curve in the tunnel. It seemed like the dragon had to angle its head back a bit to breathe fire. He prayed that observation was correct.

The dragon closed on Nathan. It saw him standing against the wall and roared. Then it cocked its head back to send the flames that would immolate him.

The creature spat out a stream of fire. It lit the tube in golden light and headed for the ceiling. Nathan dove to his right and balled himself up behind the curve in the tube.

Behind him, fire blasted the roots in the ceiling. He ducked his head as the bag of explosives disappeared into the flames. He closed his eyes and covered his head with his arms and gloved hands.

The explosion nearly deafened him anyway. The shockwave sent him sprawling against the floor. A hailstorm of rocks pelted his back and sides. He felt the heat of the flames envelop his body. A muffled dragon cry sounded from up the tube.

The rocks stopped falling and the air cooled. Nathan realized that for the second time in an hour he'd survived almost being buried alive in a lava tube. He opened his eyes to moonlight.

He stood and shook the dirt and stone from his back. He didn't feel burned, so the decades old Nomex had done its job. Turning, he saw a tree growing up from the tube and through a hole in the ceiling, as if it had sprouted like Jack's fairytale beanstalk. In reality, the blast had blown open the tunnel roof and the tree whose roots he'd passed under had collapsed into the tube. The collapse had sealed the dragon in the other side of the tube with a truckload of broken black basalt.

Nathan smiled at his amazing stroke of luck and the Providential protection of the curve in the tube. The side of his cheek stung when he did. He touched his fingers to it and they came away bloody. He wasn't quite unscathed.

He crawled up the pile of collapsed earth and along the trunk of the tree. He stepped out into a forest of tropical plants. If he was inside the park, he hadn't gained much elevation on the trip in. He pulled out his phone and hoped for signal. He got one and called up his GPS app. The signal locked and a red dot appeared inside the park's eastern edge. He zoomed out to find the spot on the map where he'd parked his car in Hilo. The terrain he'd passed under wasn't forgiving. It would be a long roundabout hike to get back to his car.

He pulled out the map he'd gotten from Suzi, compared it to his app, and marked the location of the tube collapse. This would be one place where they'd definitely be able to find a dragon. Or the place to avoid to steer clear of one in the future. He liked the second plan. He was sure that Kathy would like the first one.

Kathy! He remembered that Kathy hadn't joined them. Had she gotten there late, and encountered Suzi as she escaped her attempt to kill him? Or was she in some other awful situation?

He didn't have any texts from her. He called her number again and it went to voicemail. If someone had tried to kill him, there was no telling what might have happened to her.

He unzipped his flight suit to the waist, and set out for his car.

CHAPTER 25

Bright sunlight awakened Kathy.

Her head pounded like a giant was beating it with a baseball bat. She opened her eyes to see a blazing sun peering over the rim of the Kilauea crater. That meant she was at the bottom of it.

That realization woke her up in an instant. No one should be down here without a half-dozen pieces of protective gear, of which she was wearing none. An overwhelming stink of sulphur filled the air. She looked around to see Kilauea's lava pool a few hundred yards to her left. A billowing plume of white steam swept north of the pool. This was the most dangerous place in the park.

Despite her throbbing head, she tried to rise. She jerked to a halt halfway up. Heavy, iron shackles clamped her wrists together. A rough-finished iron chain ran from the shackles to a matching pin sunk into a boulder.

She thought back to how she got here. She remembered going out to check on her Jeep, then being attacked. She touched the side of her face with the back of her hand. It stung like hell and felt one size too big.

She looked around the barren crater for something to help get her out of this mess. Nothing, not even a stick. Just a few puddles of rainwater from yesterday's showers, and the heat of the day would make short work of them.

She noticed something else though. The ground around her was stained green, yellow, and orange, as if someone had painted a little lumpy rainbow path from where she sat straight back to the lava pool. The stains looked exactly like the ground around the off-limits steam vents along the crater rim.

Her heart sank. That trail of mineral stains said that the toxic steam plume now running to the north normally ran in her direction. She thought of all the times she'd seen the plume rise off the crater and in fact she'd never seen it travel in any direction except the path that would have it roll over her. The morning breeze would shift as soon as the sun warmed the crater's dark floor, and the toxic exhaust would head her way.

She needed to signal for help. She looked across the rim. The Jaggar Museum sat perched on the edge. But it was literally miles away. Even using the magnification viewers on the observation deck, no one would pick her tiny form out against the rock background, if they were looking in her direction at all.

The area around the base of the chain's anchoring pin was recessed, where the edges had chipped after it had been driven into the stone. Rust coated the bottom quarter of the pin. That sparked some hope. She grabbed the pin with both hands and pulled. It didn't move.

The smell of sulphur and minerals grew stronger. She looked up to see that the plume had already shifted more in her direction.

She wasn't going to extract the rod. But the base of the rod was the weakest point holding her to the boulder. If only that rust had worked on the pin a few decades longer, she could break the rod free.

Maybe she could make up that time. The rocks were coated with crystalized acids. Hydrogen chloride. Sulphur dioxide. Hydrogen sulfide. Hydrochloric acid especially would do a number on iron.

She pulled her badge off of her shirt. Then she leaned across the boulder as well as she could. With her hands clamped together, she gripped the badge and used the edge to scrape the acidic accreditation off of the rock. The crystals did not give easily.

The sulphur smell increased. Her arms began to tingle and she prayed that it was just her imagination forcing the reaction. She glanced over her shoulder. The plume had moved closer still, and that was definitely not her imagination.

She scraped faster. The tips of her fingers ached from the pressure. She packed the dusty crystal chips into the base of the rod until they made a little mound around it. The water would compact the pile as it dissolved the crystals.

The water! She had to get it out of the puddle and onto the stone. The chain was too short for her hands to reach the puddle, and the puddle was too shallow for her to cup water out of it even if she could reach it.

The world's worst idea occurred to her. But she didn't have time to think of another one. She was going to have to deliver water by the mouthful.

Kathy knelt down as far as she could. She leaned forward until her arms pulled back over and behind her head. Her shoulder sockets screamed. With an agonizing extra stretch, her lips touched the puddle. It smelled like a weak mineral bath. She sucked in a mouthful.

She nearly spit it out on reflex. It tasted awful. She shuddered as she held it in her mouth. The good news was that it didn't burn. The rain might have pooled along the floor here, but the water hadn't dissolved the hardened crystals and become toxic. She prayed it would do just that with the pulverized material she'd packed around the rod.

She crawled back up the rock, hung her head over the metal rod, and let the water dribble from her mouth. Drips hit the powder. A puff of smoke rose from the pile. Hope that this plan might work sprang to life.

She spat more water on the rod. The powder dissolved and turned into a slurry around the base. Kathy got a whiff of the mixture and it made her eyes water. The chains clanked as she fanned the fumes away with her hands. She spat the rest of the water onto the rod.

She fanned harder, but the chemical smell persisted. She looked across the crater. The strengthening smell wasn't coming from the rod. The plume from Kilauea's crater was almost on her.

The slurry around the rod turned orange. That meant that the iron rod was decaying as it reacted with the acids. She grabbed the rod and tried to bend it side to side. It didn't move.

The acid slurry bubbled. But the plume was coming faster. The sulphur fumes reached down Kathy's throat and seared her lungs. Her skin began to itch.

She dropped down on her back to temporarily cleaner air. The chain kept her hands up much higher. Mist blew over her fingers and made them burn. The plume was about to engulf her and set her whole body afire.

She raised both feet in the air and pulled the chain between them. Her pant legs slid down to her knees. She reared back and then rammed the soles of her boots against the rod. The rod didn't move and the impact made her knees sting. A second thrust did no better. She thought she was about to literally die trying to get this rod out of the stone. Mist hit her ankles and her skin tingled.

She gave the rod one last, mighty kick. The weakened iron snapped. Her feet flew across the boulder and she scraped her calf against the stone. She rolled over face down onto the crater floor and sighed in relief.

But she wasn't safe yet.

On her hands and knees she crawled south, away from the advancing plume. Her shackled hands hobbled her. Sharp, tiny stones dug into her palms and knees. The chain bounced and rattled behind her.

Yards away, the plume engulfed the boulder she'd been chained to.

Clear of the steam, Kathy rose to her feet. Her head made a swirling left-hand spin, then she regained her equilibrium. She wondered if she had a concussion. That made her even angrier at whoever had kidnapped her and left her to die by the lava pool.

She oriented herself inside the great crater. Further south there was a steep trail that led to the crater rim. When she got to the top, she'd still be in the restricted zone, and it would still be a hike to get back to a road where a visitor might give a park ranger a ride. But waiting here for a rescue would just be suicide by dehydration.

She headed for the crater wall.

CHAPTER 26

The knock on Nathan's door was accompanied by the sound of rattling chains. His first thought was of Scrooge being visited by Marley's ghost.

"Nathan, it's me," Kathy said.

Nathan bounded over and yanked open the door. Kathy looked like hell, hair askew, skin pale. Her uniform looked like it had been rinsed in some kind of mineral bath and let dry. Worst thing was, she smelled like a dozen rotten eggs. Then he noticed the heavy iron clamps wrapped around her wrists and the coil of thick chain in her hands.

"Whoa," Nathan said. "What happened to you?"

Kathy shook her head and then looked over her shoulder. She gave a forced smile and a clanking two-handed wave to an octogenarian couple in a small SUV. They smiled, waved back, and drove off. Kathy stepped inside and Nathan closed the door.

"They picked me up on the south side of Crater Rim Road," Kathy said. "It took a lot of convincing to get them to bring me here instead of a hospital." She let the chain drop to the floor. "The shackles took some fanciful explaining."

"They still do," Nathan said. "What happened?"

"I was kidnapped outside my cabin. I came to chained up near the crater. Kilauea nearly killed me." She gave the chains a shake. "How about you get me out of these?"

"Totally!"

A set of new stainless-steel bolts clamped the older iron wristlets closed. Nathan took a leatherman tool from his belt and loosened the nuts. Nathan paused to examine the wristlets and chain.

"Say, this is vintage iron, hand forged. Probably dates back to the eighteenth century. Hawaii had no metallurgy back then. This would have had to be imported." He rotated the chain upside down. "But without a slaveholding culture...say, this could have come from a whaler, converted from a slaver. The captain could have dumped the chains to save weight. If I could track down when these were made—"

"Nathan! Mind looking into that *after* you get them off my wrists?"

Nathan's face reddened. "Sorry. Right away."

He spun the nuts and popped both bolts free. He pulled the wristlets away to reveal Kathy's scratched, red wrists. She sighed in relief.

"Let's take care of those wrists," Nathan said.

He led her to the bathroom and pulled first aid materials from the medicine cabinet. Kathy began to wash her wrists.

90

"I was worried about you when you didn't show for the lava tube trek," Nathan said, "and then you didn't answer your phone."

"I was lured out of my quarters in the middle of the night. Someone big jumped me. Next thing I know, it's morning and I'm chained up by the lava pool."

"Someone wanted you dead, but didn't outright kill you. You were left as a sacrifice to Pele. Kaniela told me that was an ancient practice among the Hawaiians, to offer a sacrifice for Pele. Dying from poisoned gas asphyxiation would match that description better than being tossed in lava, and be a lot safer for the people doing the sacrifice. That explanation would also match the date of these chains."

"If I ever find out who thought I needed to be the human sacrifice, I'll make sure they have a date with those chains." Kathy patted her wrists dry. "What did you find in the lava tube?"

"A nasty bout of betrayal and a fire-breathing dragon."

Nathan relayed the story of his near-death experience.

"You were lucky to live through all that," Kathy said. "I can't believe Suzi collapsed the tube on you."

"Total bummer. These are the experiences that make me hate dating."

"What do you think the odds are that two different people try to kill both of us at the same time and are not working together?"

"Worse than the odds of me finding the chains from a New England slave ship in a Hawaiian volcano."

"Where did that collapsed tube open up in the park?"

Nathan led Kathy to his desk and pulled the map of the lava tubes from the drawer and unfolded it.

"Where did you get that?" Kathy said.

"Borrowed it from Suzi just before she tried to kill me." He pointed to the spot on the map he'd marked. "That's where I blew the tube open."

"These other lines on the map?"

"Suzi said those were tubes other cavers had mapped."

"You'd think they'd share this with the Park Service since they honeycomb park lands. Unless the people making this map were planning to use it for something bad."

"Kind of thinking killing us is something bad," Nathan said.

"What exactly was it she blew the tunnel up with?"

"Something called Ventex." Nathan also told her the other numbers that had been stenciled on the explosives that had twice almost killed him.

Kathy turned to his computer and typed the name and numbers into a search engine. The screen filled with a list of links and a few pictures.

"Found something," Kathy said.

"And got us flagged as some sort of terrorist threat at the same time," Nathan said.

She called up one of the links for an explosives manufacturer. The picture on the site was of a red container the size of a wide cigar box.

"That's it," Nathan said.

The description was of Ventex, a commercial explosive, generally used to blast rock for construction projects. There was a long list of special permits required to purchase it.

"I'm going to guess that Suzi wasn't a civil engineer for a construction company," Kathy said.

"Not that she mentioned."

"Wait, I saw something else."

Kathy hit the back button and scanned the list of links. One was to a local news story about two years ago. She clicked on the link.

The story was about a burglary of a construction site. The crew was widening the main road that led to Moana Kea. Some equipment was taken, but the police were most worried about the explosives that went missing. An undisclosed amount of Ventex.

"This isn't that large an island," Kathy said. "Big coincidence if Ventex is stolen and a separate block of illegal Ventex ends up trying to bury you in a lava tube."

"Way big, I'd say. But she stole it so that she could have it ready two years later? To bury someone she didn't know then in a tube she didn't yet know about?"

"So she and whoever she's working with stole it for some other, more immediate reason two years ago. Two years ago was when the last set of eruptions began. Let me see that map again."

Nathan spread the map out between them. There were what looked like penciled-in and then erased markings around tubes on the eastern edge of the island. Kathy pulled up a recent satellite photograph of the same area. She pointed to locations that looked like a sea of black slag.

"These are the lava fields from the last set of eruptions from Kilauea. Look at those tube ends. They are all upstream near the start of those new lava fields."

"So you think they blew open pockets of underground magma and triggered the eruptions?"

"There were a series of what the NGS called strong subsurface quakes before the lava let loose," Kathy said. "Underground explosions would look just like that. Someone with Suzi's knowledge about the subterranean could probably pull it off."

"But what's the motive?" Nathan said. "Just to wipe out some individual homes and a subdivision?"

"That's a good question. People who'd kill park rangers aren't the type to go to this kind of effort for an insurance or land scam or something like that. But we need to keep focused on the dragons. They are still in the park boundaries for now. We're going to need to put them down before they get out and overrun the island."

"Your plan?"

Kathy leaned back in the chair. "I wish I had one."

"I may know someone who can help us make one," Nathan said.

CHAPTER 27

"Who is this person we're meeting again?" Kathy said to Nathan from across her Jeep.

Nathan motioned for her to turn the vehicle up the street where the Alika leader's rundown apartment complex stood.

"Kaniela Mizuno," he said. "He's the man Butler sent me to see after our run in with Kang. His people have a history with Kilauea dragons. At a minimum, he'll believe us."

They pulled into the parking lot. Chris Lee stood guard outside Kaniela's apartment. Kathy parked and turned off the car. Nathan nodded in Chris' direction.

"He's security, but we'll be cool."

Chris scowled at their Jeep. Kathy was not comforted by Nathan's assurances. Chris approached them and Nathan rolled down his window.

"The hanale wants to know if you are here about dragons," Chris said.

Kathy punched Nathan in the shoulder for being so blatant about something supposed to be secret. Nathan turned to her.

"Ow! I didn't say anything."

"I'll take that as a yes to dragons," Chris said.

He opened the door and squeezed behind Nathan into the Jeep's cramped back seat. He had to sit in the middle to make himself fit.

"We'll go meet the hanale," he said. "I'll guide you."

Kathy gave Nathan a "what-the-hell-are-we-doing" look. Nathan shrugged. Kathy rolled her eyes and shifted into gear.

Chris directed them out of town and up through a maze of one-lane, barely-paved roads, where palm branches regularly brushed the Jeep's sides. Kathy was pretty sure they'd crossed into the Kahuku Ranch property, but the park boundaries were poorly defined this far west. All during the drive Chris deflected all questions with "The hanale will explain."

They pulled off onto a dirt trail which went straight uphill. Kathy dropped the Jeep into four-wheel drive low and began to crawl upward. A few minutes later, the trail ended. Kathy stopped the Jeep.

"We're there?" she said.

"Almost," Chris answered. "Now we walk."

The three got out and Chris guided them up a trail. Fifteen minutes in, they came to a level spot where moss and ferns covered an open area of the hillside.

"The hanale takes for granted that all you are about to hear will never be shared with anyone," Chris said.

"Absolutely," Nathan answered.

Chris stepped over to the hillside and bent down. He reached a hand under a large fern and exposed an iron pull handle. He grabbed it and yanked.

A door like on an old storm cellar opened up. Completely covered by moss and ferns, it looked exactly like the land around it. It revealed a lava tube that was over six feet tall and just as wide. Electric light shined from inside. Chris stepped aside.

"The hanale is waiting for you," he said.

"You aren't going in?" Kathy said.

"Only the hanale can enter." Chris definitely sounded like he wasn't thrilled with the two *haoles* being allowed in when he wasn't.

Kathy wasn't thrilled with the idea that Chris could slam that door shut and lay enough weight on it that the two of them might never get out.

But before she could voice her objections, Nathan strode into the tube. Given the choice between yanking him out and questioning Chris' motives, and just following him in, she opted to follow him. She was relieved when the door didn't slam shut behind them.

Unlike the other tubes she'd been in, the walls of this one were very smooth, as if all the rough edges had been sanded down. A dozen yards ahead, an old, overweight man sat on a cheap folding beach chair. He wore a faded Hawaiian shirt adorned with bright flowers. An electric lantern balanced on one of the armrests. Two canes leaned against the wall.

"That's Kaniela," Nathan whispered.

"How did he hike up here? You told me he was practically crippled."

"He is," Nathan said with amazement.

They approached the old man. He stared at them.

"Hanale," Nathan said, "this is Ranger Kathy West. She works with me."

Kathy nodded to the old man. He cleared his throat.

"You have come to believe the dragon myth?" Kaniela said.

"We've both seen them," Kathy said.

Kaniela sighed. "The Park Service knows that we still guard the Hakuna Ranch. What no one knows is that we also keep guard over the Kilauea dragons. For centuries it has been our responsibility to keep them at bay. Now, I am afraid we are about to be tested.

"I don't get out of my apartment much anymore, but a network of Hawaiians in and out of the Brotherhood keep me informed. I know about the fires in Hilo. My warriors have seen tracks and other signs in the ranch lands. All this tells me that the dragons have returned. Your actions led me to believe that you were going to try and stop them."

The old man took the canes from the wall and used them to lever himself upright. He nodded to Nathan, then to the lantern. Nathan picked it up and followed as the old man hobbled deeper into the tube. He stopped by a series of paintings on the wall.

This was no crude, Stone Age artwork. Detailed outlines had been carved into the black stone, then highlighted with paints. The result had a vibrant, three-dimensional quality. There were several scenes. In the first, a nest of red eggs sat inside a circular cavern. The eggs all stood upright, and the close-packed domes made the arrangement resemble the surface of a wasp's nest.

"The Kilauea dragons have lived here in the volcano's heart since before man walked on these shores. When all the volcanoes were active, they populated the whole island chain. But now they only survive in Kilauea. When the magma levels drop, the nest chamber is exposed, the dragons hatch, and swarm the island. Then they lay new nests where the eggs can grow fueled by the volcano's warmth."

Kathy knew of many similar examples. Cicadas were able to remain as unhatched eggs for years. Alligators depended on the warmth of the sun to incubate their eggs.

"Generations ago," Kaniela said, "it was believed that human sacrifices to Pele would convince the god to keep the dragons at bay, but it did not."

The old man moved down to the next drawing. Nathan moved the lantern closer to the art work. In it, men with spears and shields battled a Kilauea dragon as it spat a stream of fire onto them.

"It fell to our greatest warriors to defend our lands and our villages from the dragons that escaped after each eruption. Many died, but we were at least able to keep the dragons contained until the rising lava put the nest back to sleep."

"You told me everyone who faced the dragons died," Nathan said.

"A half-truth," Kaniela said. "I could not have you underestimating them."

"We've seen these things up close," Kathy said. "I shot one and it didn't flinch. How could your people survive against them?"

"Neanderthals hunted mammoths with spears," Nathan said. "Seems suicidal now, but people were definitely tougher in the past."

"And we had special weapons," Kaniela said.

He shuffled back deeper into the tube. The rangers followed and Nathan held the lantern high. Along the wall rested over ten rectangular shields like the ones pictured in the painting. Each was over five feet tall and about three feet wide. Kaniela picked one up and held it closer to the rangers. The pebbled surface looked very familiar.

"The shields are covered in the skin of slain dragons," Kaniela said. "More flame resistant than anything man has ever made. Even the dragon itself cannot bite through it. When our warriors made a wall of the shields, the flames could not touch them."

"By wedging a pattern of the overlapping curved edges against the tube walls," Nathan said, "they could create an integrated blast shield, and advance using the shields the way Roman legionnaires did."

Kaniela took two steps farther down the tunnel. He picked up a spear from a stack of them against the wall.

"Then we would kill them with these."

"Whoa," Nathan said. "That makes bullfighters look like cowards."

"If a bullet can't pierce a dragon's skin," Kathy said, "there's no way a spear could get through."

"These can," Kaniela said. "The bamboo shafts are hardened in a fire and filled with molten metals to give them strength. And they have very special tips."

He extended the tip to Nathan and Kathy. The point was several inches long, with four blades. The ends of the blades sparkled from more than just a sharp edge.

"What's in those blades?" Kathy said.

"Diamonds."

"Diamonds in Hawaii?" Nathan said.

"Diamonds are compressed deep underground," Kathy said, "and often brought to the surface through rising mantle, what we call lava once it breaks the surface. But you're right, there's no record of there ever being diamonds on the island."

"Just as there are no records of dragons," Kaniela said. "Our people can keep a secret. We know what would happen if the world knew there were diamonds here. Pele's home would be leveled."

"Don't tell me," Kathy said. "The deposit is on the Kahuku Ranch."

Kaniela smiled. "I'm sure I don't know anything about that."

"It would still take a hell of a thrust behind one of these to take down a dragon," Nathan said.

"And that is why the Alika Brotherhood must stay physically strong, ready to respond if the dragons return."

"So everyone in the Brotherhood knows this story?" Nathan said.

"No, only the hanale pass it down through the generations. The Brotherhood trains, but they do not know it will be to do this."

"Someone is pretty well versed on the human sacrifice part of it," Kathy said. "I was kidnapped and left to die chained up at the edge of the lava pool."

Kaniela's face fell. "Oh no. Some believed that Pele's anger could only be satiated with blood. There was a place in the crater where such a thing was once practiced, long ago."

"At least one person's trying to bring it back," Nathan said.

"We have moved beyond such an unenlightened view. Pele is best revered by preserving her mountain, not killing in her name. A limited few disagree."

"Anyone in particular come to mind?" Kathy said.

"Kang, the man who threatened you at the ranch's edge. His beliefs are a throwback to old ways, driven by a hatred of others instead of a love of the land."

"He seems to know a lot for one who is not hanale," Nathan said.

"Kang's father and I grew up together," Kaniela said. Disappointment tinged his voice. "The crater was our playground, Kahuku Ranch our hangout. His royal bloodline was not as strong as mine, but we learned about the ways of our ancestors together. He was destined to have a high position in the Brotherhood.

"But he did not see our role as defending our lands and heritage in a world among many cultures. He didn't see Hawaii as a land that had accepted waves of newcomers before we were born and would do so long after we were gone. He saw the island as something owed to him, almost personally. Anything that went wrong in his life was the fault of others, especially the *haoles*."

"From our brief encounter with Kang," Kathy said, "it seemed like he passed that attitude down to his son."

"And then Kang amplified it. After his father's death, I kept him in the Brotherhood, knowing that it was the anchor he needed to keep the storm inside him from sending him far from shore. But it wasn't enough. Kang is out to avenge his father's death. It isn't beyond him to try to kill you, or to even let the dragons loose to wreak havoc on the island."

"We think that someone used explosives to trigger the recent eruptions," Nathan said. "That would lower the lava levels in Kilauea, perhaps enough to expose dragon eggs for hatching."

"That would be a catastrophe," Kaniela said.

"We need to stop them," Nathan said.

Kathy pondered how much of their secret mission mandate to share with Kaniela. "But we can't get the Park Service or the public involved. If word got out, the whole park would turn into a battlefield."

"I agree," Kaniela said. "If the secrets of Kilauea are exposed, the last bits of our ways here will be gone forever. My people will fight these dragons."

"We'll do it together," Kathy said. "If the lava level drops are recent, there may not be a lot of dragons loose yet. I mean, if there were, there would have already been sightings everywhere. Nesting reptiles are territorial, defensive of their unhatched brood. If we can find and destroy the nest, no more dragons are hatched. And attacking the nest should draw the remaining dragons back to defend it."

"So we're going to charge through lava tubes to subdue fire-breathing dragons with nothing but shields and spears?" Nathan said.

"And our courage and honor," Kaniela said.

"Not thinking that's going to tip the scales much," Nathan said.

"The first question is how do we find the nest?" Kaniela said. "Our Brotherhood treats the tunnels as sacred. We don't go in there, have no maps."

"We can help with that," Kathy said. "We have a map."

"Awesome," Nathan said. "This morning, as I was climbing out a lava tube after being attacked by a dragon, I was thinking how great it would be to give that experience another try."

CHAPTER 28

Kaniela told them it would take some time to assemble his warriors for combat. He would have them ready by sundown. Kathy and Nathan hiked back to the Jeep and then drove back to Kathy's quarters.

Once there, Nathan gave Kathy the Nomex flight suit and helmet he'd taken from KMC.

"It's fire retardant," Nathan said, "not fire proof. But I'm sure that dragon would have baked me alive if I hadn't been wearing mine."

"At any rate," Kathy continued, "you're going to need a way to defend yourself down there. The old man in the Hawaiian shirt might put a lot of faith in his diamond-tipped spears, but I don't."

"Aloha shirt," Nathan corrected. "No self-respecting islander calls them Hawaiian shirts."

Kathy rolled her eyes. "Whatever. We can't go down there with nothing but Stone Age weapons."

"And you suggest?"

Kathy took her service weapon from her holster and laid it on the table.

"I'll give you my pistol and I'll use my backup. Bullets don't penetrate the dragon's skin, but a shot into soft tissue like the eye or mouth would *have* to do some damage. Plus, Kang and anyone working with him sure won't be bulletproof."

"Not that comfortable carrying a gun," Nathan said.

"I wish you'd already taken the NPS firearms certification course, but I'll give you the basics so you don't shoot me instead of the dragon."

Nathan's face went white and his chin trembled.

"I'm sorry," Kathy said. "I don't really think you'd shoot me."

Nathan stepped over to the table and stared down at the gun. His face looked somber, his eyes distant.

"I have to admit something," he said. "I haven't even filled out the paperwork for firearms certification."

"Are you serious? Knowing the kind of creatures we are likely to be up against at any park we go to? You have to arm yourself."

"I can't. More precisely, I won't."

Nathan pulled a chair away from the table and sat down. He stared off to Kathy's right at someplace far away that only he could see.

"Even as a kid," he began, "I was a history nut. Totally obsessed. I mean, once my friends and I, we went skateboarding at an abandoned factory. I ended up exploring the architecture and digging for artifacts.

"So, I'm nine, and a friend of mine, Jessie, tells me that his father has a German Luger that his grandfather brought back from Germany in World War II. I talk him into getting it and bringing it outside. He doesn't want to, but I like browbeat him into it, call him names, you know how kids are.

"So he brings it out and hands it to me. A Luger is a very distinctive gun, had a real evil vibe to it, or at least I thought so as a kid. But still, it's like the coolest thing ever. I imagine some German Army officer holding it up over his head as he surrendered to American soldiers in France.

"So I start playing around with it, the way kids play with toy guns, pointing at things, pretending to shoot things. Jessie gets all worried that we're going to break the gun. It's solid metal, I say, there's no way to break it. And then to prove my stupid point, I drop it on the ground.

"And that's when it went off. Neither of us had checked to see if it was loaded. The bullet rips through the poor kid's foot, severs two toes. Blood's just pouring out of this big hole in his shoe and I'm standing there in shock, watching. His mother comes out panicked and screaming. I become terrified and start bawling. Then there's an ambulance in the driveway, then come the cops."

Kathy was afraid to ask for fear of the answer. "Was Jessie okay?"

"He didn't die. But two toes were gone. He never walked normally after that."

"And what happened to you?"

"No criminal record, chalked up to stupid kids and parents without a gun safe. But I became the talk of the school, and even more of an outcast. My fascination with history continued, but I had a new aversion to guns. Even now…"

With his finger, he nudged the pistol on the table a few inches farther away from him.

"…that one gives me the creeps."

"Oh no," Kathy said. "And I joked about you shooting me. That was so awful of me."

"You couldn't know."

Kathy returned her pistol to its holster. "Then guns are out of the picture for you."

Nathan's face brightened. "But I might have a weapon that works even better."

He got up from the table and stepped over to something narrow and a few feet tall under a sheet.

"Correct me if I'm wrong, but that dragon's skin is excellent at shedding heat, but probably very poor at getting warm."

"Living its life in and around volcanoes it's not going to be adapted at all to cold."

"That's why I made this."

With a theatrical flourish, Nathan pulled the sheet from the device in the living room. It looked like a small, silver skin diver's tank with a compressor on the bottom. An insulated hose protruded from one side with what looked like a bug sprayer wand at the end.

"Which is what?" Kathy said.

"It delivers a stream of frozen carbon dioxide."

Kathy eyed the contraption over. The way the different pieces were grafted together made her think of some kind of mechanical Frankenstein's monster.

"When did you turn into a mad scientist?"

"After a dragon tried to broil me in a lava tube. But I can't take credit for all of this. The tank and compressor were supposed to be for the KMC walk-in cooler, but it didn't come with the right connectors. But I will take credit for weaponizing it. See, I was inspired by flamethrowers used in World War II. Then my research showed they were also used in World War I. But the real mindblower is that the first use came from...drum roll please...the Chinese. Of course. See, in 919, the Song Dynasty was battling the Mongols—"

"Can we stay on track here, Nathan?"

"Whoa, yeah, totally. So this will compress the carbon dioxide into a liquid gas, then I can direct the stream at a target using the wand. It's got a range of about fifteen feet."

"That's pretty close when we're icing fire-breathing dragons."

"But nowhere near as close as the Alika Brotherhood have to get to use their spears."

"That's true."

"And you can't keep the thing blasting too long. The wand starts to freeze up..." Nathan rubbed his hand hard and fast against his leg, "...and then your hand does, real quick. But you shouldn't need to fire it long. It will freeze living skin on contact. My biggest fear is that it will flash freeze the dragon too quickly, the creature won't feel it, and it will just keep coming. I want this instant ice bath to send the dragon running."

Two shoulder straps hung from one side. Kathy scooped them up in one hand and lifted. The contraption weighed over fifty pounds.

"It's man portable," Nathan said.

"If a gorilla is in the family of man, then yes, it is."

"I think I can carry it," Nathan said.

There was more hope than certainty in his voice. Kathy looked over Nathan's skinny body. She was surprised he'd even manhandled the thing into his quarters.

"I'll take it," she said. "You handle navigating with your map. And I like you as the go between for me and Kaniela. Seems like you've won him over."

Nathan tried and failed to mask looking relieved. "What else could we use going in there?"

"What *could* we use? Heavy-duty fire suits like I saw smoke jumpers use in Angeles National Forest. I'd like more protection than the Nomex suits give. But finding and borrowing two sets would raise a lot of questions from wherever we got them. And the lava tubes are too tight in places to get through wearing all that."

"And the Alika Brotherhood might be righteously peeved if we didn't bring enough for everyone."

"As to weapons? You've probably concocted our best hope. I don't think anything short of high caliber military guns will get through dragon skin. But even if we somehow borrowed some machine guns that no one will miss, there's the danger of blasting away inside those fragile tubes and burying ourselves."

"It's as if the natives had already thought these things through centuries ago," Nathan said, "and settled on shields over bulky personal protection and the precision of diamond-tipped spears over massive force. I could give you a long list of all the times solutions the earliest inhabitants had for local problems still end up being the best ones in the present day."

"So looks like we go in with what we have," Kathy said. "Kill the dragons, then freeze-dry the eggs."

"Easy as a walk on the beach," Nathan said. "What could go wrong?"

Kathy's phone dinged. She checked the screen. The text was from Superintendent Butler.

"Where the hell are you?"

"We may have trouble at the office," Kathy said.

CHAPTER 29

"Where have you two been?"

Superintendent Butler looked furious as he stood behind his desk and stared down Kathy and Nathan.

"Well," Kathy started, "the fire investigation at that bar took a long time."

"That was over a day ago."

"Well, there was a lava tube that opened up under the house. But we inspected it, and it was completely dormant. No liability at all for the park."

"Who's the *we* doing that inspection?"

Nathan gave a sheepish grin and raised his hand. "That would be me."

"What the hell? I thought I was specific about you sticking to your assigned duties. There were three missed interpretives at Jaggar Museum and you were supposed to lead all three."

"That's on me," Kathy said. "I didn't want to go into the tubes alone. Nathan knew an experienced caver. He brought her down to the lava tube to introduce us. She recommended a group of three was safer, and in we went."

"I don't give a damn about your excuse. The bottom line is the park mission did not happen three times yesterday because Ranger Toland decided to do what you told him to do instead of what I told him to do. Does that sound like a good course of action, Ranger Toland?"

"No, no it does not," Nathan said.

"And it's going to reflect on your review," Butler said. He looked at Kathy. "Both of your reviews. I was two rangers short when you two got here. I'll be damned if I don't feel like I'm still two rangers short. Maybe more than that with all the extra work you've caused. Which reminds me, are all the Alika Brotherhood feathers unruffled?"

"Totally copasetic," Nathan said. "I can honestly say we are on the road to working better together than ever before."

Kathy had to bite her lip to not laugh.

"Well, great. One thing in a row that you haven't screwed up." Butler sat down and scribbled some notes on a pad. "Seriously, you two are each one mistake away from reassignment out of this park. We have a lot of space, a lot of visitors, and a lot of dangers. I need to trust that you're out doing your assigned duties. One more violation of that trust and you'll be shoveling out the latest mudslide on the Kalaupapa Pail

Trail on Molokai waiting for your terminations to come through. Am I clear?"

Kathy and Nathan nodded.

"Then get the hell out of here and go to work."

Kathy and Nathan left the headquarters building and returned to her quarters.

"I can't blame him for being pissed off," Kathy said. "I'd be if I were in his position."

"You'd think we could at least inform the park superintendent about our secret mission, about the danger of, oh, say, fire-breathing dragons wandering the island."

"We are following the same instructions that have kept the secret of the Park Service's founding since the start. Honestly, there's no telling how Butler would react if he knew the unbelievable truth. Right now, we need to find where that nest might be."

"Where would we look?"

"If Kang and Suzi blew holes in the volcano to drain the lava, we need to find the empty space that flow left behind."

Kathy went to her computer and called up the secure Park Service database. From there she followed a link to the National Geologic Survey database about Volcanoes National Park. The NGS had a series of studies posted about the magma levels and flow out of Kilauea. Kathy pulled up the summary.

"There was significant subsidence along Kilauea's slopes after the 2018 eruptions," she read. "That means magma levels within the volcano dropped. There are several areas here that ground penetrating radar identified as new voids. Any of these could be where the exposed nest might be."

Nathan took out the map he'd gotten from Suzi and spread it out on the table. He penciled in a rough estimate of the tunnel he'd explored outside Hilo.

"A dragon came down this tube and burned down that bar," Nathan said. "Not to mention trying to turn me into a Nathan-kabob. And that tunnel leads back in that general direction."

Kathy circled a spot on the map west of Nathan's tunnel. "The NGS survey puts a significant void right about here."

"That tube might go straight to it."

"We can enter where you escaped," Kathy said. "It's inside the park, so we can get there without involving any outside authorities. We'll clear enough debris to get in the tunnel, then follow it to the nest, and destroy it."

"I'll give Kaniela and the Brotherhood the location. When do we go?"

"If we don't keep our park assignments today, Butler will have search parties out hunting us, and we don't need that. But we don't know Kang's timetable, so sooner is better. Kaniela said he'd be ready tonight so we'll hold him to that. We'll go in at dusk."

CHAPTER 30

"It isn't working," Kang said.

Kang and Suzi stood on the ledge overlooking the nest cavern. Portable lights lit the area in a bright white. The space was the size of a football field. Before the eruptions had drained it, the pool of lava had made the cavern too hot for anyone to enter. Even now, the room had only cooled to a sauna-like level.

At the cavern's far edge, a pulsing glow lit the floor by the cavern wall. Just contained by the raised earth around the edge, the newly exposed nest of the Kilauea dragons throbbed with life. Hundreds of eggs stood packed in a near-perfect formation.

A vent in the cavern roof drew the more noxious fumes up and out of the area, but the scent of sulphur still permeated the air. The stiflingly humid cave was warmer than the last time Kang visited, and the reason was obvious. Off to the left, a pool of magma crept higher, millimeter by millimeter.

"This whole cavern was dry last time I was here," Suzi said.

"And at this rate, the rising magma will re-cover the eggs and send the dragons back into stasis before they hatch."

"The magma is upwelling faster than our openings are releasing it. You just can't trust a volcano."

"Does this seem funny to you?" Kang said. "All of our work is about to be undone."

"Relax. We'll just release more lava. There are three blast locations we planned that we didn't use. The one on the park's south side is closest to where the magma is pooling. I can blow that open and it should at least keep the level from rising."

"You have enough Ventex or did you use the last of it failing to kill that park ranger?"

"He's dead and buried. Trust me."

"If he was, the news would have been full of a missing park ranger story. It isn't."

"I held up my part of the deal And I killed him in a lava tube collapse that looks like a natural event. You, on the other hand, told me you left a kidnapped Ranger West chained to a rock in the crater like you're some Batman supervillain."

"You wouldn't understand," Kang said. "If we want Pele's blessing, we have to earn it, sacrifice a life to her."

"According to you, that sacrifice didn't really come off that well."

"I was watching from the crater rim. It was too far away to see exactly how she got free, but the chain must have broken."

"That kind of public execution might be tough to explain," Suzi said. "Don't get me wrong. A lot of people are going to die to give the island back to nature. But until the dragons hatch, you might want to keep a lower profile. What do you think would have happened if the police were called in to investigate a dead ranger chained to a volcano?"

"Nothing at all if we had Pele's blessing."

"Whatever. Look, I'm going to get the lava flowing downstream. Don't kidnap anyone while I'm gone, okay?"

Kang just glared at Suzi. She retreated down the tube.

He'd met her at a protest on Mauna Kea. The skinny white girl had joined the native protest to protect that sacred ground from development. She didn't think the land was sacred, just that all development everywhere should be stopped and then reversed.

People like her always made him laugh. Mainlanders who flew in and thought they needed to be the voice of the Hawaiians. The implication that his people could not speak for themselves was insulting.

He was ready to tell her to get off his mountain, but then he overheard her brag about how she'd sabotaged a pipeline project. She'd worked at a coal mine, and managed to tuck away a bit of explosives for herself now and again. When she'd amassed enough, she set three charges at pipeline junctions. Boom, boom, boom. Workers panicked. Construction stopped until a massive security force could be brought in.

That was just the kind of skill he'd need for his plan. He spoke with her privately several times after the protest and found she was more than talk. She was ready to take action. She'd been caving the tubes on the island a while. He filled her in on his plan. She agreed to help before he even finished telling her the details.

The young *haole* was little more than a means to an end. She knew the lava tubes and she knew her way around explosives. Otherwise he'd have long ago offered her to Pele instead of the park ranger.

She thought they shared the same goal, but Kang knew that she mocked Kang's belief in Pele. She thought nature could continue without the gods behind it. *Haole* beliefs.

When the dragons were free, he'd let her see the purge they made of the non-native islanders. Then of course, she'd have to be consumed as well. Though her heart might be in the right place, her bloodline could never be. But until then, she would be quite valuable.

CHAPTER 31

Nathan stood with a binder in his hands at Byron Ledge overlooking the secondary crater of Kilauea Iki. This long-dormant feature was miles south of Kilauea's main active caldera. Beside him, a sign marked the 1959 Kilauea eruption. The picture showed plumes of lava sailing high in the air. A class of schoolchildren and their teacher stood in a semicircle around him.

"Over sixty years ago," Nathan said, "an eruption filled this entire crater, turning it into a lava lake."

Several excited kids whispered about how cool that would be.

"And some super awesome lava plumes shot almost two thousand feet into the air." Nathan opened his book filled with pictures of tourists at the lava flows. Many were dangerously close to the molten rock. "The lava lake was a major tourist attraction while it lasted."

"Can we get that close to some lava?" one boy asked with way too much enthusiastic expectation.

"No, the park has much stricter rules now. And there isn't any active lava where you will be hiking. But rainwater does seep into the cracks in the ground, touch hotter rock, and turn into steam. You'll see steam coming up from the ground in some places."

One girl raised her hand. "Where did all the lava in the lake go?"

"Super good question. It drained back into an underground pool in the volcano."

"Will it come back up?"

"Maybe someday, but not today."

"Are there dangerous animals in the crater?" the boy who wanted to see lava asked.

Sure kid, fire-breathing dragons are ready to jump from lava tubes and send you all screaming. "No, the crater is safe."

"Okay," the teacher said, "thank the ranger for telling you about the volcano."

The kids responded with a chorus of "Thank you, Ranger Nathan." Then the teacher shuffled the kids off to the trail for the long climb down to the crater below. As they filed down, a call crackled over Nathan's radio.

"Need a ranger response to reports of a visitor vehicle in the Mau Loa restricted area southwest of Chain of Craters Road."

Nathan shook his head. Too many people assumed that having four-wheel drive meant that the driving restrictions didn't apply to them.

"Vehicle is a light blue Subaru Outback."

Nathan's heart jumped. That description matched Suzi's car.

He'd tried calling her after the incident in the lava tube, hoping to talk her out of whatever plot she was involved in. But the calls had gone straight to voicemail. Now he had to assume that if she was driving off-road in the restricted area, she was taking another step closer to releasing the dragons.

He grabbed his mic. "This is Toland. I'm in the area and will check it out."

"Roger that."

Nathan wasn't at all in the area. But if that was Suzi, he wanted to be the one to find her. She had a lot to explain.

He jumped in his Park Service truck and headed out of the parking area at a speed that would have earned a visitor a traffic citation. He turned the truck south and gunned it.

He tried to make a plan about what he'd do if Suzi was out there. Was he going to hold her there while he called in the police? What could he tell them? He had no proof that she'd been in the tunnel with him. He didn't think anyone had seen them arrive at the burned-out bar. Proving that the tube had been blown up would be possible, but he guessed the kind of forensics work to sniff out the explosive residue would be time consuming. With the allegations just being his word against hers, the police might not even take any action.

The hopeless romantic facet of his personality still thought he might turn this around. After all, he liked her. He thought she'd liked him. Hadn't there been some kind of spark between them? He nurtured this unrealistic hope that she wasn't really aware of what she'd gotten into, that there was a benign explanation for the Ventex charges in the lava tube. Maybe somehow her involvement had been a mistake, and he'd get her to see the light.

A few minutes later he arrived at the Mau Loa restricted area. On the left, scrubby trees and bushes sprouted up the road's edge. On the right, a solid field of black, dried lava stretched out to the horizon. Just under a mile away sat Suzi's Subaru Outback.

Nathan sagged back against the seat. He was afraid there'd be no good outcome from what he was about to do.

Still unsure of what he was going to say when he confronted her, he dropped the truck into four-wheel drive and headed toward the car.

And he needed the four-wheel drive. The truck's big tires intermittently slipped against the slick basalt. He could keep going forward as long as he kept his speed low.

But losing traction was the least of his worries. While this open plain looked like solid rock, there was no telling what was underneath. The place could be honeycombed with gas bubble voids and lava tubes. The weight of the truck might punch it through the surface and into a chamber who-knows-how deep.

But he had to take those risks. He didn't have time to turn tracking Suzi down into a twenty-minute walk, only to have her drive away from him before he got to her.

As he closed on the vehicle, he realized one of his suppositions was wrong. Just north of her car, wisps of steam wafted out of tiny vent holes. This field was more active than he'd thought. That guaranteed an unstable surface.

He stopped the truck near Suzi's car and got out. He peered in through the open passenger window. She wasn't inside. But on the passenger seat was a GPS device, a map, and something that looked like the controller for a toy radio-controlled car.

Then he saw Suzi, crouched over what looked like a bore hole. Just a bit of the excavated rock dotted the ground around it. Apparently it had been dug a while ago, and the extracted stone had been spirited away to someplace else. Without that telltale debris, the hole would have been invisible unless someone was right on top of it.

Nathan caught his breath. Beside Suzi sat a familiar looking rectangular package. Sadly, at this point in life, Nathan recognized Ventex on sight. Silver duct tape bound a black box with a short antenna to the explosives.

"Suzi!"

She startled and looked up from the hole. "Nathan? What are you doing here?"

"You mean like, instead of being buried alive?"

"Well," she said as she stood up with the explosives in her hand, "for starters."

"I used your second charge to blow a hole in the lava tube and escape before a dragon roasted and ate me."

A smile broke out on her face. "I'm so glad. I was so frightened. There was an explosion in the tube that sealed it off. I assumed you were dead...was afraid to go to the police...I mean we were sneaking around; we weren't supposed to be there in the first place. What a relief that you are okay."

Nathan so much wanted to believe her, and so much couldn't. "So you didn't try to seal me in the tube?"

"Nathan! God, no! Why would I do that? Someone must have planted the explosives before we got there, trying to kill you, or me, or both of us."

"Suzi, you're holding the same explosive in your hand right now."

She looked at the device in her hand. The concern on her face melted away into a sly smile. "So it is. Well, I gave that story a shot."

"You need to put that down and walk this way. That area is totally unsafe. There's subsurface magma everywhere."

"Well, duh. That's kind of the point. I need to give this volcano another enema before the magma backs up and re-covers the dragon eggs. Don't want the little ones going back to sleep before they hatch."

"Why would you want to hatch fire-breathing dragons?" Nathan said. "Thousands would die."

"You of all people should understand. You're a ranger. Don't you want this park to encompass the whole island, to have the land be the way it was before people spoiled it?"

"No, I don't. The Park Service mission is to preserve things as they are, not to turn back time to the Jurassic Era. And after the dragons wreak havoc and kill thousands, the government will come in with overwhelming force to destroy them and all this will have been for nothing."

"Are you kidding me? No they won't. People like me stop dam construction to save snail darters. Animal rights movements will make the Kilauea dragon their poster child and demand that they be given the island. Scientists will side with them for the research opportunity. Hawaii and insurance companies will agree because none will want to pay to fix this place after most of it is burned to the ground. Then these things will breed and when the population peaks, they'll do what Komodo dragons do. Swim to a nearby island for fresh territory. And we'll do this whole thing all over again on Maui. You should be helping me realize the dream instead of trying to stop me."

Suzi's plan was crazy, but with just the right amount of internal logic to make a crazy person believe it.

"Not going to happen," Nathan said.

He reached into her car and pulled out what he now understood to be the bomb's remote detonator. He threw it to the ground and then stomped on it. It shattered into pieces.

"And now you can't set off that charge. This is over."

"Silly boy. I just can't set off the charge remotely." She pointed to a switch on the bomb controller. "I can just throw this switch and, boom, instant eruption."

"You'll be killed."

"No, *we'll* be killed. But I'll go out making the world a better place, and you'll die trying to stop me. Both our stories get a perfect ending. Bye bye, Nathan."

Suzi threw the switch. A red light on the box lit up and she dropped the charge down the bore hole.

CHAPTER 32

The charge exploded underground with a muffled boom. Dust and stone blew straight up out of the bore hole and the concussion sent Suzi flying backward. She landed on her back.

The ground beneath him shuddered and Nathan fought to keep his balance.

The wisps of steam rising from the vents grew into thick, hissing jets. A spider web of cracks spread across the ground all around the bore hole. The dark recesses of the cracks began to glow red. Nathan backed away.

Suzi sat up. Blood trickled from her ear. She looked around her and laughed.

Then a plume of lava blew up from the bore hole like a geyser. Globs of glowing lava rained down around the bore hole. Golf ball-sized chunks splattered Suzi. Her laughter turned into shrieks of pain.

The glowing cracks widened and then chunks of black stone between the gaps sank into a surging sea of orange lava. The slab where Suzi sat dipped forward and dove into the pool. She scrambled for the high side of the slab. The stone sank. The lava swallowed and silenced her.

A gas bubble rose from the lava's surface. It burst and sent a blast of sulphurous heat into Nathan's face. More globs of molten rock sailed out in all directions. Some landed just short of Nathan's feet.

He ran back to his truck and jumped in. He looked out in time to see the flowing lava run into the tires on Suzi's doomed car. They burst and then the car rolled sideways into the deepening pool. The gas tank exploded in a yellow ball of flame. Flying shrapnel pitted his windshield with a series of sharp, staccato cracks.

Nathan dropped the truck into reverse, looked out the back window, and hit the gas hard. All four wheels spun and the smell of burning rubber filled the cabin. The truck didn't move. He looked back out front.

This wasn't the usual slow-moving Kilauea lava flow. Suzi had blown open an area with significant back pressure. This lava was surging.

He let off the gas and then goosed the truck once. The sticky tires grabbed the ground. He raced toward the road. But the lava was moving faster.

He gave it more gas. The truck accelerated but warning lights inside flashed as tires alternately spun and gripped the ground. The truck braked and jerked as the anti-lock system tried to make sense of the insanity.

The lava closed to a few yards away. Nathan switched off the traction control and accelerated. The road was still far away. The truck swerved right and left as the tires slipped and regained purchase. The speedometer rose.

But not fast enough. Nathan looked out front. The leading edge of the lava had disappeared under the hood. A glance out the side confirmed that the lava was under the truck. Near suffocating heat and fumes filled the cabin.

Twin booms sounded from the fender wells as the lava's heat boiled away the front tires. The truck collapsed on the rims with a jolt. Spinning steel edges gouged earth and the truck slowed. Nathan would be sitting in lava in seconds.

He jerked the truck from four-wheel drive to two. With all the power going to the rear wheels he stomped the gas pedal to the floor. The rear wheels spun and then caught. The tires dragged the inert front end of the truck forward and away from the lava's leading edge.

The truck accelerated as it slid down the black stone. Then the tires blessedly touched the pavement of the road. Nathan spun the wheel to back the truck uphill and out of the lava's path. The vehicle fishtailed back and forth, carving deep ruts into the sandy soil on both sides of the road. Finally, he regained control and pulled the truck far up out of the lava's downhill path. The front bumper scraped along the pavement and the truck ground to a stop.

The lava flowed downhill past the vehicle. Nathan took a few deep breaths to calm his racing heart. Then he stepped out and checked the truck.

The front bumper hung by a few bolts, the rims were mangled discs, and the ground-down frame of the vehicle sat on the pavement. He was no insurance adjuster, but he guessed the phrase "total loss" was going to apply here. He was going to have to call, get the road officially closed, and get a tow truck to haul the truck away.

How would he explain what he'd encountered? He looked out at the flowing stream of lava. Suzi and her car were gone. He'd tell Kathy everything, but the rest of the world would hear that he showed up and the surging lava caught him by surprise. If the report of a blue Subaru Outback had been true, it must have left before he got here.

This was a lot of lava draining out of the underground reservoir he'd just been telling those schoolkids about. That would drain the pocket he and Kathy had identified even further. And Suzi had said the uncovered dragon eggs were ready to hatch.

He and Kathy were suddenly on a much tighter timeline.

CHAPTER 33

Kang smiled as he watched from the ledge above the dragon's nest. The lava in the cavern was receding. The *haole* girl had done her job. He grabbed his spear and shield and descended to the nest.

The top half of the glowing football-sized eggs stuck straight out of the nest like the bulging cells of a bee's honeycomb. They might not have been covered by lava anymore, but they seemed nearly as hot. Kang had to use the shield to block some of the heat radiating from the pulsing eggs. He moved as close as the temperature would allow. The shells were nearly translucent. Inside each, a small, black shadow of a Kilauea dragon squirmed.

A tragedy had been averted. With the eggs so close to hatching, there was no telling what would happen if they were inundated with lava. Would they go dormant again, or this late in the game, be destroyed? He didn't know. No one knew. All the Alika Brotherhood understood about dragons came from apocryphal lore and cave paintings. Not exactly vetted scientific research papers.

It was a moot point. Now they'd all hatch, and the island would be teeming with the flaming bastards. Then mankind could begin its retreat from Hawaii.

As if sensing someone was close to the nest, a dragon stuck its snout out of a connecting lava tube on the right side, on the ledge above the nest. Then a larger dragon stuck its head from a tube on the ledge's left side. Red tongues flicked out to taste for an intruder. Heads turned and the dragons spied Kang. As one, they roared, and then attacked.

They leapt down from the ledge and crashed into a clear part of the nesting area. Kang retreated until his back was almost against the wall. He held the shield across his body so it did not block his view of the oncoming dragons. He gripped the spear tight.

The larger dragon closed quickly, with the smaller one right on its tail.

Kang raised the spear and ran to the larger dragon. The diamond blade sparkled in the light. The dragon dug in its claws and skidded to a stop. It twisted its head and revealed the scar across its blinded eye. The dragon behind it bumped into its larger brethren. It spied the spear and scrambled backwards.

Kang stepped forward. He swept the spear point's edge across the stone floor and sent up a shower of sparks. The dragons flinched.

"You think you're bad asses," Kang said, "but you know who the real Alpha male is down here."

He pointed the spear at the half-blind dragon. It shied away.

"Especially you, Akamu."

Kang smacked the shield with the side of the spear a few times. Like lions before their tamer, the dragons reluctantly backed away.

"You afraid of me? You maybe hate me, Akamu?"

The dragon grumbled. Kang's blinding of the largest dragon had cowed the rest into submission as well.

"Well, soon you and all your children can take that anger out on the people that have stolen your island from you. I'll let you loose to kill them all." He slammed the shield again. "But you'll always bow to me."

The dragons took another step back. Kang moved sideways to the stone stairway he'd descended into the nest area, always keeping the spear up and his eyes on the dragons. Like a lion tamer, he knew ferocious eye contact helped keep these creatures at bay.

When he got to the ledge, he surveyed the nest area. The dragons had crawled over to the glowing eggs. They flicked their tongues across the tops. The tiny dragons within bounced inside the eggs at the touch.

It won't be long, Kang thought. *Pele's children will hatch, and the island of Hawaii will return to its wonderful natural state, with me as their king.*

CHAPTER 34

"You're sure we're not going in there alone?" Kathy said.

"Kaniela said the Brotherhood would be here," Nathan said.

He and Kathy stood beside the opening Nathan had blasted into the roof of the lava tube during his dragon escape. Kathy tightened the Velcro straps at the end of the flight suit sleeves over the sage green matching gloves.

"We already had a brush with dragon's breath," she said. "These heat resistant suits aren't one use only are they?"

"As long as they aren't burned," Nathan said. "I guess."

"You guess?"

"There really aren't instructions for fire-breathing dragon use."

The sound of feet crunching on the trail drew their attention. Chris Lee stepped out into the clearing, followed by two other Alika Brotherhood members, both even bigger than Chris. All three carried dragon-skinned shields and diamond-tipped spears.

Two more large members of the Brotherhood appeared. They carried a sedan chair made of two bamboo poles and a woven wicker platform with a seat that resembled a kayak. Kaniela sat up in the seat, three spears by his side. Each of the bearers carried a shield strapped to his back.

Kathy thought that sedan chair explained how the old man had gotten up to the dragon-slaying arsenal in the cave days before.

When the men arrived at the puka, they lowered the sedan chair to the ground. Levering himself up with a spear, Kaniela rose. He stepped over to Nathan and Kathy and stuck the base of his spear into the ground.

"The Brotherhood is here to perform our sacred duty."

"Five men against who knows how many dragons?" Kathy said.

"These are my strongest warriors, the best trained. The tubes are narrow, and too many warriors would work against us. And there aren't five." Kaniela raised his spear across his chest. "There are six."

"You plan on going in?"

"This is the sacred mission the Brotherhood was created to fulfill. Royal blood must lead the combat."

Kathy was about to say that there was no way in hell she was letting him slow them down when they took on the dragons. Nathan touched her shoulder and stepped forward.

"*Hanale*," he said. "I've been in these tubes. Some of the passages are wicked tight. Six hunters may be too many."

Kaniela's eyes narrowed. "And you think the old man should stay behind?"

"I think history's full of examples of leaders who were great because they trained their men well for the fight ahead. Very few of them led the men into battle."

"That is not the way of my people."

"Think of those people, the others in the Brotherhood left behind today," Nathan said. "What if you are killed? What if all of us are killed? Is there someone ready to take your place, to organize a second attack if this one fails?"

"We won't fail."

"We might," Kathy said. "Dragons, cave-ins, lava, toxic gas, Kang. There are lots of ways to die down there. Do you want to risk the future of the Brotherhood?"

Chris stepped up to Kaniela.

"*Hanale*, the Brotherhood needs you alive. We both know there is no one ready to take your place, no one who knows our oral history as you do. Leading this attack? I can do this. Leading the Brotherhood? Only you can do that."

Kaniela opened his mouth to protest, but then closed it and said nothing. He turned to Nathan and handed him his spear.

"They won't let you down," Nathan said.

"If I didn't already know that," Kaniela said, "I would not agree to stay behind."

Kathy shouldered the backpack CO2 compressor. There was no way Nathan would be able to lug this into the tube. He already had a climbing rope across his chest and two harnesses hanging from his belt in case they needed to rappel down to the nest area. Those seemed to weigh the ranger down more than enough.

"Let's get going," she said.

"My men will lead," Kaniela said. "They will block the tube with their shields if a dragon appears, then advance with their spears."

Kathy shook her head, and started to say that men with shields facing down fire-breathing dragons was stupid. Nathan's touch on her shoulder cut short her objection.

"Remember," he whispered in her ear, "traditional practices become traditions because they work."

Kathy tapped Nathan on the chest with the CO2 wand. "I'm still bringing our new tradition, just in case."

"No issues with that at all."

"Our history says that the dragons can only breathe so much fire," Kaniela said, "the way a snake only has so much venom. It takes a few minutes for the dragon to recharge after an attack. But don't be fooled. It will eat you whether it cooks you first or not."

Nathan turned to the rest of the group. "The explosion collapsed part of this tube. We'll need to clear ourselves an entrance."

"Not a problem," Chris said with a smile.

The five men pulled headlamps from their pockets and strapped them to their heads. They snapped on the lights and climbed down into the collapsed tube. Working together, they cleared all but the largest rocks from the lava tube in a few minutes. Chris came back up above ground.

"There's enough room to get by," he said.

"Kaniela," Kathy said. "If we aren't back in two hours, something went very wrong. Assume the worst. Make a new plan."

"We'll be back before that," Chris said.

"Indeed," Kaniela said. "The Alika have never failed to protect the island. Kang believes that Pele is on his side, but she is not. You will be victorious."

Kathy preferred to not rely on the intervention of a volcanic goddess. "Let's go wipe out that nest."

Chris and two brotherhood members headed down into the tube. Kathy and Nathan followed, and the last two men brought up the rear.

The men had cleared enough space to enter the tube, but just barely. The barrel-chested Brotherhood members tore their shirts as they squeezed past sharp rocks. Kathy had to drop the CO_2 unit, slip through the space between boulders, and then pull the unit by after her. Once the team was all in, Kathy looked back at the jagged slit of moonlight that marked the passage back to the open world. Up ahead was only darkness. And dragons.

"Let's go," she said.

The three Brotherhood members took the lead and the group moved out under the fuzzy glow of their headlamps.

"How far up from here did you get?" Kathy asked Nathan.

"Not much further than this, then the dragon dropped in."

As they advanced, the air warmed and the humidity rose. The smell of sulphur and minerals grew stronger. The tube curved to the left, which should have been toward the potential nest site. Kathy checked the compass attached to her wrist. The needle slowly spun in a circle.

"Nathan, Kilauea's churning magma is playing hell with the local magnetic field."

Nathan already had the caver's map in his hand. He annotated a position in pencil. "I can still give us a rough location keeping track of our steps and direction, as long as things don't get too hairy down here."

Something hanging from the wall caught her eye.

"Hold up," she said.

The group stopped. A few square feet of a papery, almost transparent sheet hung from the wall. She carefully removed it and turned it over. Chris and Nathan came to her side.

"What is it?" Nathan said.

Kathy pressed what she'd taken from the wall onto the face of Chris' shield. The patterns made a roughly accurate match.

"Shed dragon skin," she said. "Lizards molt and scratch off old skin on rough surfaces. These dragons must do the same. They regularly use this tube. We're on the right track."

"I'll pretend that's good news," Nathan said.

Kathy's light played across a human shoeprint in the sand along the base of the tube. The imprint was big, with almost no tread pattern. It didn't match the soles of her boots, or the shoes of the three Alika who'd led the way. Kathy pointed it out to Chris and Nathan.

"We aren't the only people down here," she said.

"Even the dedicated lava tube explorers haven't discovered this tube," Nathan said. "It isn't on the maps."

"And the Brotherhood has stayed out of the tubes until now," Chris said.

"Except for Kang," Kathy said.

The situation may have just taken a turn for the worse. Kang releasing the dragons was bad. Being able to walk among them and possibly direct them would be catastrophic.

She hoped this team was prepared for that.

CHAPTER 35

A few minutes later, the team came to an intersection in the tube. A smaller passage broke to the right. Chris turned to Kathy.

"Which way?"

"Take the bigger tube. It's still heading to where we think the nest is. Right, Nathan?"

Nathan angled his map for a better view under his headlamp. "As far as I can tell."

Chris led the men down the larger tube. Nathan and Kathy passed by the left-hand branch.

Suddenly a blast of flames rocketed out of the smaller tube. The tunnel lit up bright orange for yards in all directions. Intense heat threatened to sizzle Kathy's back. The stream of fire slammed into the wall of the main tube. Flaming liquid splattered the arm and chest of one of the rearguard Alika. He dropped his shield and spear and screamed in terrified agony.

Chris responded in a flash. He barreled between Kathy and Nathan and sent them flying against the tube walls.

A dragon's roar echoed from down the smaller tube. Then its head popped out into the main tube, lit up white in everyone's headlamps. Kathy flicked the power switch on the compressor on her back and it hummed to life.

The burning man staggered back the way he came and dropped to the ground. The other rear guard and Chris raised their shields and converged on the dragon from two sides. Its mouth opened to reveal rows of sharp, white teeth.

But the passage was too narrow for the dragon to turn and face the men. Its head slammed into the wall to the right, then left, unable to directly face either man. It roared again in frustration.

Chris and the other Alika put all their weight behind their shields and crashed into the sides of the dragon's head. Chris thrust his spear under the shield with a long, underhand swing. The diamond blade pierced the dragon's neck with ease. A gusher of red blood splashed against the floor of the tube.

From the other side, the Alika guard's spear point flashed in the lamp light as it swept up under the dragon's head. The point buried itself just behind the dragon's jaw.

The dragon screamed and slammed its head up hard into the tube ceiling. A spray of rocks showered the ground. Both men dropped their shields, grabbed their spears with both hands, and slashed.

Two great rends opened in the dragon's neck. A torrent of blood drenched the floor and the men's feet. The dragon's eyes rolled up in its head. A single puff of flame wheezed from its mouth and dissipated before hitting the wall. The men pulled back their spears and the dragon fell to the floor, dead.

Chris stood over the dragon's corpse, panting. Thick veins in his neck throbbed. His knuckles bleached white as he gripped the spear. He shook himself free of the spell of combat.

"Hold this position," Chris ordered.

The two guards up front faced down the tube with their shields blocking the way. The surviving rear guard stood beside the dragon corpse and kept watch down the left-hand tube, though nothing larger than a mouse was going to squeeze past the dead dragon. Chris headed down the main tube to the burned Alika.

Kathy killed the compressor. "Keep a watch here," she said to Nathan.

Nathan nodded and moved to the left-hand tube. Kathy followed Chris to the injured man, who sat on the ground against the wall. They knelt beside him.

Burns covered his chest and left arm. What remained of his shirt appeared fused to his skin. Tears streamed down his face as he fought back the pain.

"Gilbert, my brother," Chris said. "You are stronger than the pain."

Gilbert bit his lip and nodded. "I'm sorry."

Chris shook his head. "No, I should have checked the side tunnel as we passed it. It's my fault. Now there's nothing more you can do here. Go back, see a doctor. Get those burns treated before they get infected."

Gilbert managed a weak smile. "I'll tell the doctor my propane grill flared up."

"Those things are so dangerous."

Chris helped Gilbert up and handed him his shield and spear. Gilbert held both in his good hand and then limped off down the lava tube.

"We were lucky," Kathy said.

"No," Chris said. "That was how our people have always fought the dragons. In the tunnels, where their size works against them, not above ground where it works in their favor. We have practiced those attack moves for generations, not knowing how we would use them. I know how now. The moves all came back to me when we started to fight, like turning on an automatic pilot."

"But we are one warrior short."

"I'll send one man from the front to the rear and take the lead myself. We can still do this. We have to."

***

Kaniela sat on a fallen branch at the collapsed roof of the lava tube. Clouds obscured the moon and the breeze accentuated the night's chill. He checked his watch for the hundredth time and swore that it must have stopped at one point. There was no way time could be passing so slowly.

This was not what he'd been born to do. He hadn't lived his life so that he could wait in safety while the Brotherhood he led battled the dragons of Kilauea. It was another dishonor, heaped upon Kang's humiliation of him in his own home. Why, twenty years ago, or even ten, neither of these things would have happened to him. Back then he'd still been strong, able to hike the length of Kahuku Ranch in half a day, able to stand toe-to-toe with the Brotherhood's greatest warrior. Now what was he? A broken old man, waiting for the real warriors to return home in a victory he could not share.

A moan came from the tube entrance. Kaniela used a stick to rise to his feet. He shined a light at the opening.

Gilbert staggered up out of the tube, barely holding his shield and spear in one hand. The opposite arm looked badly burned, as did half his chest. Kaniela went to him. Gilbert dropped his weapons and bowed his head.

"We were ambushed by a dragon," he said. "The thing caught me before I even knew it was there. All I saw were flames."

"The rest of the team?" Kaniela asked.

"They're okay. They sent me back and they are going on to the nest."

Kaniela thought that going forward one person short was a bad idea.

"Get back to the car," Kaniela said. "I need to get you to the hospital for those burns."

"I can make it to the car alone," Gilbert said. "From the car, I can call one of the brothers to get me to the hospital. You stay for the team's return."

"Are you sure?"

"Yes, *hanale*. My mistakes should not be your problem."

Gilbert headed down the trail to the car. Kaniela looked down at the spear and shield on the ground.

He could not let his people go into battle a man short.

He hobbled over to the spear and picked it up. Then he grabbed the shield with his other hand and held it up against his shoulder. How many times over the decades had he held these weapons in the secret cave, longing for the chance to fulfill his destiny and defend the island from the dragons of Kilauea? Fate had now offered him that opportunity. He took a headlamp from his pocket and strapped it across his brow.

Using the spear as a cane, he went to the opening in the ground. He took a deep breath and then began to pick his way down the jumble of rocks into the darkness below.

CHAPTER 36

Kathy and her team advanced up the lava tube. The increasing heat and intensifying smell confirmed they were getting nearer to the heart of Kilauea. Nathan made another check of the map.

"We have to be very close," he said.

Up ahead, claws scraped stone in the darkness.

"Cover!" Chris ordered.

Kathy and Nathan ducked down. Chris and the Alika up ahead in the tunnel dropped their spears and blocked the tube with their overlapping shields. And not a moment too soon.

A wall of fire came sweeping down the tube. It crashed into the shields and both men rocked back at the force. Flames licked around the shields' edges and the back sides glowed red.

But the shields held. The flames died away and a dragon roared.

Kathy switched on the compressor and the CO2 unit hummed to life. The two other warriors turned to guard the rear from a possible second dragon attack.

The dragon charged Chris' position. It slammed into the shields and pushed both men back several feet across the sandy floor. That left their spears on the wrong side of the shields.

Nathan charged forward with his spear. He jammed it through a slit between the shields. The dragon screamed. Then Kathy dashed up.

"Give me a gap!" she said.

Chris moved his shield a few inches to the side. Kathy got a full-on view of the Kilauea dragon, just a foot from her face. Its red eyes blazed with hatred. It opened its mouth and inhaled to roar.

Kathy pointed the CO2 wand inside and pulled the trigger.

A misty blast filled the dragon's mouth. The creature made a dry, gargled croak. It scurried backwards.

The men lowered their shields for a better look. The dragon staggered, then made a series of desperate inhalations, as if all the oxygen had been sucked from the tunnel. It dropped to the ground, moaned, and went still.

Everyone in the party froze, as if waiting for some inevitable last gasp attack from the creature. None came. The men completely lowered their shields.

"You killed it," Chris said.

"I think the CO2 froze its lungs," Kathy said. "It suffocated."

"Any win is an awesome win at this point," Nathan said. "Any chance there were only two dragons down here?"

Both Kathy and Chris looked at him like he was crazy.

"I was afraid that would be your answer," he said.

They climbed over the dragon and resumed their push forward. Minutes later, the tunnel opened up to a ledge overlooking a crater. Man-made lights around the edges lit the area. Chris was the first to the edge. He dropped his shield and his jaw hung open.

At the far end, the nest of eggs glowed red, as did the surface of the wall behind it. Far to the left, a pool of lava lapped at the cavern's far edge.

"That glowing collection over there sure looks like eggs," Nathan said.

This was what they'd been searching for, the dragon's nest. They had to destroy it immediately. But Kathy could not help but be awestruck. The scientist in her marveled at this, the only nest of the only examples of dragons left on Earth. But for the sake of mankind, this nest had to be the last.

"That's our target," Kathy said. "This depression was a magma pool before the eruptions drained it out."

She moved to get to the edge of the ledge. Chris held her back with a hand against her shoulder.

"Let's make sure we're alone," he said.

They waited a few minutes, but heard nothing.

"We're running out of time," she said.

Chris gave the cavern another worried appraisal. "Okay. Let's go."

From the ledge, Kathy could see a series of rocks that could work as steps down into the crater. They looked too regularly spaced to be natural, and she imagined that Kang had stacked them there for his frequent forays down to check on the eggs.

"Nathan, looks like we won't need your rope after all."

Nathan dropped the heavy coil and the harnesses on the ground. "Awesome."

She led the group to the steps, and minutes later they'd scaled down into the crater. Chris and Kathy led the group across the slick crater floor to the glowing nest. Hundreds of football-sized eggs stood on end, packed together.

The wall behind it also pulsed a dull red. One of the Brotherhood stepped over and touched it. He yelped and pulled his hand away.

"Probably a magma chamber back there," Kathy said. "I'd stay clear of it."

The eggs glowed from underneath. The shells were just opaque enough to glimpse the writhing black silhouettes of tiny Kilauea dragons.

"They look fully developed," Kathy said. "Ready to hatch."

"Not so threatening when they're small," Nathan said.

"Reptiles mature quickly, and if they can breathe fire at birth, hundreds of small flamethrowers crossing the island might be worse than a few large ones. Even if we could kill the young easily, would we ever hunt them all down?"

"We'll finish them now, while it's easy," Chris said.

He raised his spear and drove the point down onto one of the eggs. The point hit the shell with a crack. But the shell didn't break.

Chris tried again, harder. Again, the shell held. The surface didn't even chip.

"Shows you how strong the little ones are," Kang's voice boomed across the crater.

The group looked up. Kang stood on the ledge near where they'd entered the nest area. He held a diamond-edged spear in one hand. A pistol rested in a holster on one hip.

"You can't break their shells," Kang continued, "but very soon they'll easily emerge from them. Even hatchlings can belch enough fire to burn down a house and bite hard enough to rip a man's leg from its socket."

From the tunnel behind Kang came a furious war cry. He whirled around just as Kaniela emerged at a limping run, spear raised for the attack.

"Kaniela, no!" Nathan screamed.

The old man didn't have the speed, or the reflexes to match Kang. As the *hanale* charged, his former protégé easily sidestepped the attack with a hop to the left. With a quick upward swing, he struck Kaniela's spear with his own. The weapon flew out of the old man's hands and bounced over the ledge.

Momentum moved the old man past Kang. Kang spun his spear like a twirler's baton and then cracked the base of it against the back of Kaniela's head. Kaniela dropped and hit the ground face first. Kang drove a foot down into Kaniela's back and lay the tip of his spear against the base of the man's neck.

"There's a difference between brave and stupid, old man," Kang said. "Your time in charge is officially over."

Kang raised the spear and drove it down into Kaniela's back. Blood spurted from the wound and the old man screamed. Then he went limp.

"Bastard!" Kathy said. She drew her pistol and took aim at Kang.

Then dragons roared around them.

The sound seemed to come from everywhere at once. Kathy scanned the crater and saw nothing.

"Oh, yes," Kang said. He pulled the spear from Kaniela's lifeless body. "Forgot to mention that nesting adult dragons are very territorial. You really should not have messed with the eggs."

Then dragons appeared. Three heads popped out of lava tubes around the crater's edge. Red tongues slithered out to taste for prey. All three heads swiveled to lock eyes on Kathy's party. The largest of the dragons was blind in one eye.

This was the kind of battle the Alika said they could not win. Out in the open, where the dragon's speed and mobility gave it every advantage.

And Kang stood in front of the only route to escape.

CHAPTER 37

Kathy reached back to turn on the compressor. But Nathan had beaten her to it and the machine spun up to speed.

"Out of the crater!" Chris ordered.

The group broke into a mad dash for the makeshift stairway to the ledge. With a roar, the three dragons pursued. The two smaller dragons ran out ahead, as if in a competition to impress the one-eyed dragon.

The humans were not going to win this race. One of the Brotherhood turned just as a dragon reared its head back to spit fire. He screamed, ducked down, and covered himself with his shield.

The dragon snapped its head forward and exhaled a blast of fire at the crouching man. The flames bounced off the face of the shield. But the volume was too great. Fire surged around the sides and dove inward in its quest for more oxygen. It swept over the Brotherhood member's feet.

Flames raced up his legs. He cried out, dropped his shield and spear, and tried to beat out the flames with his hands. The dragon charged, its meal unguarded. Its jaws opened, and aimed to swallow the flaming man.

Chris tossed away his shield and sprinted forward to his brother's defense. Just feet from the dragon, he hurled his spear at the creature's open mouth. The spear flew true and the point buried itself in the dragon's upper pallet. The creature wailed. With an angry sweep of its head it struck the warrior and sent the burning man sailing across the crater and into the wall.

Still on the run, Chris scooped the man's abandoned spear from the floor. He slid head-first along the smooth crater floor and under the dragon's head. With a mighty thrust, he plunged the spear into the dragon's chest. A waterfall of blood gushed down over Chris. He rolled out from under the beast.

The dragon staggered. Chris jumped up and grabbed the shaft of the first spear sticking from the roof of the dragon's mouth. He drove it upward into the dragon's skull. The dragon wailed and dropped to its side.

The second dragon had taken on the other two Alika warriors. In an amazing show of courage, they did not panic, but moved in opposite directions to the dragon's sides. The dragon had to choose a victim, and turned to face the warrior to its right. It sent a ball of fire in the warrior's direction. It sailed just off target and his shield protected the man from the flames.

But the attack gave the second warrior his opening. He charged at the dragon's exposed side. He thrust his spear into the dragon's body just behind its front leg. The spear went deep and the dragon roared in anger.

As it turned its head back to the second warrior, the first charged in from the other side. He jammed his spear into the dragon's side in the center of its ribcage. Blood spurted from the wound.

The dragon screamed and began a furious right-hand spin as it craned its neck to bite at the first warrior. But the man grabbed hold of the protruding spear and held on to stay out of the dragon's jaws.

The other warrior released his spear, but his fate was sealed. As the dragon spun, its tail swept him across the cavern. He skipped once and then slammed into the cavern wall. He didn't move.

The dragon whirled across the cavern floor, gnashing its teeth at the warrior who hung to the spear shaft, just out of reach. It made a concerted, frustrated lunge at just the wrong moment. It lost its footing and skidded into the lava pool at the cavern's end. The dragon and the warrior burst into flames and became ash.

The largest dragon had its sights set on Kathy and Nathan. Being half-blind didn't seem to hinder it. It headed straight at them. It reared back its head to immolate them.

Kathy's heart raced. She felt defenseless, staring down a dragon pointing the flimsy CO2 sprayer in its direction. The thing would burn her to a crisp before it got into range.

Nathan appeared at her side, carrying Chris and the other Alika's shields. He closed the shields over their heads like a tent and pulled her down to her knees. Kathy squeezed next to Nathan. The shield edges touched the ground.

A stream of fire blasted them. The pressure drove the shields down onto their heads. The dragon skin covers glowed and in an instant the air around them went from warm to broiling. The compressor sounded like a jet engine as its whine echoed inside the tiny space. Flames licked in around the shield's lower edges.

The firestorm stopped. The dragon was out of juice, but it had to be close by. Kathy saw her opportunity. She jumped up from between the two shields with the sprayer extended.

The dragon *was* close. Closer than she'd expected. Its head wasn't somewhere in front of her, it was right beside her. Fury filled its one, red eye.

With a sideways sweep, it knocked Kathy up and out from between the shields like removing a splinter. She flew across the crater and hit the ground, shoulder first. A flash of pain reverberated all the way down her spine.

But the dragon wanted Nathan. Its jaws yawned open and then snapped closed around the two shields with Nathan sandwiched between them. His head and one arm hung out from the shields just below the dragon's jaws. His eyes were wide with terror, his mouth opened in a silent scream.

The dragon was having trouble crushing the shields, whether due to the Brotherhood's proven design or the strength of its ancestor's skin. The compressor on her back still hummed. Kathy pointed the wand at the dragon and...the trigger was gone. Torn away when she hit the ground.

She dropped the wand and pulled her pistol from its holster. She couldn't pierce the thing's skin, or even draw its attention with the 9 MM. But as every parent warned, with a careful shot, she could put an eye out.

She lined the dragon's blood-red eye in her sights and squeezed the trigger.

The pistol boomed in the closed cavern. The bullet found its mark. It burst the dragon's eye in a shower of viscous liquid.

The dragon roared in agony and dropped Nathan. Its head twisted around as the blinded beast tried to find its assailant. Its forked tongue slithered out to taste for Kathy's scent.

She aimed and fired again.

The second round tore through the base of the dragon's tongue. Bright red blood splattered the dragon's snout. Its tongue went limp and then retracted into the dragon's mouth like a piece of spaghetti.

Now with nearly no senses, the dragon stomped and twirled in frustrated rage. It roared and sent a spray of blood across the crater floor. Nathan jumped up from between the crushed shields and ran for Kathy. The dragon charged away from them. As it passed, its sweeping tail missed them by a foot. It ran so hard headlong into the wall that Kathy thought it had to have broken its neck. But it was only stunned. Then it followed the crater's wall until it found a lava tube. It scampered in and disappeared.

From up on the far ledge, Kang cursed in frustration as the last of his dragons met defeat. Kathy turned and aimed the pistol at him, but it would be a tough shot at this distance.

She didn't get to pull the trigger. Kang hit a switch on the wall and killed the lights.

Darkness enveloped the cavern. The only illumination was the glow of the nest of eggs, and the duller glow of the cavern wall behind it.

"Nathan?" Kathy called.

"Right here." He arrived at her side. She could barely make out his face in the weak light of the nest.

She tried to turn on her headlamp. Nothing. Her fall must have broken it. "Are you okay?"

"Considering that I was almost the filling for a dragon's Oreo cookie, I'm awesome. You?"

Kathy did a quick self-diagnostic. "Battered but not broken."

"I wonder if anyone else—"

Off to the left a headlamp blinked on.

"Kathy? Nathan?" Chris called.

"Coming to you," Kathy said

She and Nathan walked over to Chris. He stood beside the dragon he'd slain. He pulled his spear from the creature's mouth. Another light came on and the other surviving member of the Alika Brotherhood limped over to join them. His face was drawn and pale in the light of his lamp.

"Donovan, my brother," Chris said. He clapped him on the shoulder with a smile and then looked past him into the darkness. "And Scott?"

Donovan shook his head.

"Then it is just us," Chris said. "You're okay?"

"Twisted ankle. Nothing more. You saw what happened to Kaniela?"

"And Kang will pay for that as soon as we get out of here."

From the direction of the nest came a sharp crack.

"Hell no," Kathy said.

"Go up on that ledge and find the light switch Kang turned off," Chris said to Donovan. The man nodded and limped to the steps in the wall. He began a labored climb, favoring his twisted ankle.

Kathy led them to the glowing nest. Just as they arrived, the cavern lights came back on. She unshouldered the CO_2 machine and set it aside.

The dragon silhouettes practically bounced inside the eggs. Cracks laced the surface of several shells. An irregular window a few inches around had opened up in the top of one egg. The dragon inside pressed the tip of its snout through the hole and burped out a small ball of fire.

"We're too late," Kathy said.

CHAPTER 38

Nathan jumped back from the nest. He'd had more than enough dragons today, even small ones.

"Whoa," he said. "The dudes are born breathing fire."

Chris raised a spear and plunged it through the hole in the egg. The dragon screamed. Chris gave the spear a twist and the dragon stopped moving.

"And from the feel of it, they are still bulletproof," Chris said. "If these get out, they'll devastate the island."

"We'll make sure that they don't," Kathy said.

"And just how are we going to do that?" Nathan said.

"We'll figure it out. Chris, you need to help Donovan get out of here. If we fail, someone needs to warn the world about what's coming."

Chris handed Kathy his spear. "I can send more members of the Brotherhood once we get out."

Kathy looked at the squirming dragons in the eggs. "By then it won't matter."

"Then we'll stop them at the pukas from the tubes."

"Who knows how many different tube exits there are from here," Kathy said. "You won't be able to guard them all. Give us an hour. If we aren't out by then, you can try your best to keep them contained, but warn the world that dragons are coming."

Chris nodded and ran for the steps to the ledge. When he got to the top, Donovan slung an arm across Chris' shoulder and the two disappeared down a lava tube. Nathan was glad they were getting to safety, but that meant it fell on Kathy and him to destroy this nest.

"Now what's the plan?" Nathan said. "We can't try to spear them all as they hatch. All it would take is to miss one and we're beef jerky. The CO_2 unit's broken, but we wouldn't have enough CO_2 to freeze them all anyway."

"These eggs are well past any stage where they could go back into stasis. This is the rare occasion where a lava flow would solve a problem."

"You sure lava would kill them?"

"They can live near it. But we saw lava burn that dragon alive. Nothing can survive being covered in it."

Nathan pointed to the glowing wall behind the nest. "We have plenty of lava on hand."

"Except that the wall has no spigot."

A tidbit of history sparked an idea in Nathan's mind.

"We can make one with this." He tapped a toe against the CO2 generator. "Cold will turn the rock holding back the magma brittle. Then a sharp strike will shatter it. There's a theory that the Titanic's steel had a manufacturing flaw that did the same thing when it struck the iceberg. We break the wall, we flood the nest."

"Except the compressor trigger's broken."

Nathan bent down and inspected the spray wand. "Yeah, it is. But with both hands you could still get the mechanism to work."

"And swim with the dragons when the lava comes flowing."

"Okay, there's *that* going against the plan."

"Unless we do it from the ledge," Kathy said. "We use the climbing rope and harness. You lower me down. I freeze-dry the wall. You haul me up before the levee breaks."

"That's a bad idea," Nathan said.

At their feet, another egg cracked open with a snap.

"But I don't think we have time to come up with a better bad idea," Nathan added.

Kathy grabbed the compressor and they ran for the steps. They made it to the ledge and sprinted for the spot over the nest. They approached where Kang had murdered Kaniela. Nathan looked away as they passed the body. He'd have to process all that later.

They got to where Nathan had dropped the rope and harness. He retrieved them as they passed. They stopped at the spot over the nest. It was only a few feet wide. A quick search confirmed that there was nothing to tie the end of the rope to. Kathy began to strap on the climbing harness.

"You're going to need to kind of feed the rope to me with it running across your lower back," she explained. "Just feed it out to me a bit at a time to lower me down."

Nathan sighed. "I can't believe I'm saying this, but I need to be the one to go down."

"What?"

"I weigh less. You can pull me up faster than I can pull you up. I understand the compressor and sprayer better than you. Wall demolition needs to be my job."

Kathy bit her lip. "I'd like to argue with you, but everything you said makes too much sense."

"Lucky me."

She handed him the harness. Nathan started to put it on. She stopped him.

"And since every second counts," she said, "you should probably go down headfirst."

"No way."

"Headfirst means that you are clear of the lava with my first pull. Feet-first means the flow might hit you from the knees down."

"I hate it when awful ideas make sense."

Nathan took off his headlamp and put it on Kathy's head. Then he strapped the climbing harness on upside down over his shoulders and across his chest instead of around his waist. He tightened it until he could barely breathe. Kathy tied on the end of the climbing rope. Nathan turned the compressor on and it whirred to life. He clamped both hands on the wand and squeezed the wand in an odd way with a few fingers. A blast of CO_2 shot out of the spray wand. He took a deep breath.

"Let's go."

More eggs cracked from the nest below them. Another tiny ball of exhaled fire rose up and burned itself out.

"Just step to the edge and lean out," Kathy said. "I'll let you down easy."

Nathan stood at the precipice. It protruded a foot or two out from the wall underneath. The crater stretched out below, the floor littered with two dead dragons and a dead Brotherhood member. All that sacrifice couldn't be in vain.

More cracking noises came from the nest. A tiny dragon roar echoed in the crater.

He leaned out over the edge. The rising heat from the eggs and the wall streamed by him and sent beads of perspiration down his face. He got ninety degrees out and grasped the straps of the compressor and the wand in both hands. The compressor hung straight down.

"Doing okay?" Kathy said.

"Hanging over a boiling hot nest of hatching dragons. Totally awesome."

Kathy fed out more rope until Nathan hung upside down. The humming compressor dangled below him. Blood began to rush to his head. If the heat didn't cook him, it felt like the pressure would pop him.

"Hurry," he croaked.

A few feet at a time, Kathy lowered him down. The glowing part of the wall moved closer. The crater floor was yards away.

The nest crackled like gunfire. Nathan looked over to see two dragons burst out of their shells. He was just over the rosy section of stone.

"Hold it!" he shouted.

He stopped moving. The nylon rope crinkled as the heat began to affect it. He squeezed the trigger mechanism. Nothing happened.

A dragon roared again.

He readjusted his grip and squeezed harder. A blizzard of CO_2 blasted from the nozzle. He pointed it against a glowing part of the stone. The pressure pushed his body away and he struggled to keep the spray hitting in one location.

The hatched dragons sprinted out of the nest toward Nathan.

The stone began to look lighter as the CO_2 froze the outer layer. Nathan moved the wand to widen the spray area.

"Nathan," Kathy called. "Dragons underneath you."

"Got it."

One dragon spat a puff of fire in Nathan's direction. It sailed past his head and blew out.

Then the other dragon jumped. It bumped into the swaying compressor. If it hit the switch and turned the thing off, Nathan couldn't restart it.

With a snap, a crack formed in the stone. Then another. Nathan aimed the wand closer to the crevice.

The other dragon leapt. Its front claws caught the cooling fins on the compressor. Suddenly the pack weighed twenty pounds more. Nathan's arms stretched in their sockets and his grip on the straps loosened.

Another crack cut across the bleaching stone. Time to break the dam.

But he couldn't swing the compressor against the wall. The extra weight of the dragon and the growing weakness in his arms was too much.

The CO_2 stream fizzled out as the tank went dry.

The dragon's rear legs scraped against the bottom of the compressor as it sought purchase to make a climb.

Nathan was out of time.

"Swing me," he yelled up to Kathy. "Against the wall."

The rope rocked and Nathan swung away from the wall. The pendulum effect sent the compressor and its dragon rider further out. Nathan swung back into the wall and the compressor came in harder and faster. It hit the wall near the cracks and sent shards of stone flying. The dragon squealed and held on tighter.

Kathy swung him out and again he guided the compressor in. It struck the same spot. More chips flew. A jet of steam blew out of the crack and grazed his shoulder. It felt like being branded.

"Again!"

The rope pulled him away from the wall. On the return, he used all his remaining strength to swing the compressor as hard as he could. It hit the wall with a boom. A jet of lava shot out of the crack and swept away the compressor and the dragon. It shrieked as it fell into the nest.

Nathan jerked sideways as Kathy pulled him away from the wall. The section he'd been over collapsed into a waterfall of yellow, molten rock.

Nathan traveled sideways and up. Then he felt Kathy grab him at the climbing harness. He reached over and helped her pull him to the safety of the ledge.

And that safety wouldn't last long. The air had turned broiler-hot in an instant. Lava rushed from the hole in the wall and inundated the nest. Eggs popped as the contents boiled. Gushing lava touched the dragon corpses in the crater and they burst into flames.

The stone beneath the rangers cracked.

Kathy and Nathan jumped to their feet and bolted for the lava tube. The ledge where they'd been standing collapsed. The lava waterfall widened and the crumbling ledge expanded and followed inches behind them as they ran. They jumped over Kaniela's body and into the tube. The rest of the ledge collapsed and the hanale's corpse slid into the growing lava pool below.

The heat became unbearable. The two dashed up the tube as fast as the light of Kathy's headlamp would allow. They jumped over the head of the dragon the Brotherhood members had slain. Eventually a point of light shined up ahead.

"Kathy?" Chris shouted.

"It's us!" she said.

They made it to the opening in the tube and climbed. Chris helped Kathy and Nathan up out of the tunnel. Donovan sat nearby on the downed tree trunk. False dawn broke at the world's eastern edge.

"You did it?" Chris said.

"We reflooded the chamber with lava. Nothing survived."

"Except Kang," Nathan said. "And we lost Kaniela's body and the others."

"They will forever be part of the place they lived to protect," Chris said. "There can be no better burial for them."

Nathan liked that way of looking at it.

"I'll go tell the families of their sacrifice," Chris said. "Then we will find and deal with Kang."

"We'll take a breather and then follow you back," Kathy said.

Chris and Donovan headed back down the mountain.

"I wonder how much of this we'll need to tell anyone at the park?" Nathan said.

"None would be my favorite answer there. But then, we need to make certain that Kang doesn't get away. The Brotherhood may be slow to act as they deal with Kaniela's death."

"Where do you think he'd go to hide out?"
"The only place we saw him hiding out before."

CHAPTER 39

A few hours later, Kathy and Nathan hurried down the trail near Kahuku Ranch. She figured that Kang, defeated and furious, wouldn't go home after escaping the lava tubes. That's where the Alika Brotherhood would begin the hunt for their traitorous former member. He'd go someplace he was comfortable, someplace he could rest under the world's radar. That would be at the ranch where he'd grown up, and more specifically, she hoped, at the cave he'd excavated to open up a lava tube to the nest.

Kathy had parked her truck at the trailhead and now she and Nathan were hiking the trail to Kang's secret cave. The two hadn't taken a break since entering the tube last night. They were a mess, wearing torn uniforms, sporting singed hair, and liberally speckled with dragon's blood. Most of all, they were tired. Kathy's feet felt like lead and if she closed her eyes, she was certain she'd be asleep in an instant. She needed the power of adrenaline to keep her going just a little longer.

She carried her sidearm in case Kang decided to surrender the hard way. Nathan had grabbed a machete from the back of her Jeep. She was proud of how the skinny historian had acquitted himself in the dragon's cavern.

"I was thinking," Nathan said. "If we find Kang, what do we do with him?"

"Arrest him. We have that authority in the park."

"And turn him over to who? The local police? The FBI? Neither of those options keeps Kilauea dragons a secret."

"We can press charges for stealing the explosives, for starting an eruption. No one would believe him if he started talking about dragons."

"The evidence of that, if any is left, points more to Suzi. And I'm not sure that starting an eruption is like, a real crime. I mean, it should be, but do you think anyone ever passed a law against it?"

Kathy doubted it. Nathan had a good point. What would they do with Kang? She hoped that Deputy Director Leister, who sent them on this secret mission, had a way to tie up loose ends like this.

Minutes later, they arrived at the lava tube puka. They crouched down behind bushes where they had a view of the entrance. The area was quiet, save for the chirp of some insects.

"You know," Nathan said, "during World War II, Japanese soldiers used caves like this as defensive positions. It usually took Marines with flamethrowers to—"

"Not really helpful right now," Kathy said.

"Right. Sorry."

The only way to find out if Kang was in the tube was to go into the tube. Kathy drew her pistol and headed for the entrance. Nathan followed behind her with his machete at the ready. They were still yards from the opening when Kang's voice boomed out of the darkness.

"Stop right there."

The two rangers froze.

"Before you do something stupid," Kang said, "look behind you."

Kathy looked around. At the base of a tree behind them sat a red block of Ventex. A black box with a short antenna was wire-tied to the explosive.

"Oh hell," Nathan said.

Kang stepped out of the shadows and into the light. He held a black box that looked like a controller for a radio-controlled car.

"Suzi's detonator looked just like that," Nathan said.

"So much as twitch," Kang said, "and boom. There won't be enough of you left to test for DNA."

Kathy's grip tightened on her pistol.

Kang moved his thumb to over a switch on the box. "You think you can quick draw on me before I can push this button, Ranger? Please try. I'm begging you."

Kathy had to admit she would not win that contest. She relaxed her right arm and moved her finger off the trigger.

"We knew you'd be hiding out here," she said. "Every branch of law enforcement is coming right behind us."

"I knew the two of you would come looking for me here. That's why you're standing in a blast zone. And I know you don't have any cavalry on the way. Except for a few idiots from the Brotherhood, the two of you have been out here with no backup at all from the beginning. No reason you'd call in reinforcements now, not when you think all you're facing is me."

"It's over," Kathy said. "Suzi died releasing the lava on Kilauea's south side. The dragons that attacked us are all dead. The nest is flooded with lava, the eggs destroyed. You've lost."

"Only this round. I found that dragon nest, maybe I can find another. Maybe there's one under Mauna Loa, or at Diamond Head in Oahu. Or now that I've mastered the art of triggering eruptions, I'll just have Pele and Kilauea turn all Hilo into slag. I have a lifetime ahead of me to find a way to cleanse these islands."

"We'll spend our lifetimes stopping you," Kathy said.

"True," Kang said. He raised the detonator over his head. "But your lifetimes are measured in seconds."

A dragon's roar bellowed out of the cave behind Kang. A rush of air ruffled his hair and he flinched. He whirled to face the cave.

The head of the blinded dragon shot from the cave's recesses. Its jaws opened to reveal the stump of its severed tongue. Two sets of razor-sharp teeth snapped closed around Kang's midsection. He dropped the detonator and screamed.

The dragon took a step outside the puka. Kathy dropped to one knee and put the dragon in her sights.

But the creature had no intention of advancing. Instead, it snapped its head up and tossed Kang up into the air. He sailed up and then fell straight down into the dragon's gullet. He was still screaming as the dragon slammed shut its mouth and swallowed.

Then too quickly for either ranger to react, the dragon darted out, spun around, and dashed back into the puka. The retreating sweep of its tail crushed rock around the puka. The scratch of claws on stone grew softer as the dragon withdrew back into Kilauea's depths.

Nathan dropped down and sat cross-legged. His machete hit the ground with a thud.

"Seriously," he said. "I'd planned on this Park Service job being way more history-focused."

Kathy went over to the detonator. A red light glowed over the switch that Kang had been ready to press. She had no idea how to disarm it.

"We'll walk that thing out of range," she said, "then come back and disarm the Ventex."

She took a few steps into the cave. A backpack lay open on the ground. A box of energy bars and packs of instant coffee sat inside atop a jumble of crumpled papers. Kathy pulled out the papers.

The pages had been printed on an inexpensive printer that left long, black streaks through the faded letters. She unwrinkled them one by one.

The first page was a set of handwritten instructions on using Ventex. She figured they were from Suzi.

The next few pages were details about the dragons. The latitude, longitude, and depth of the nest. A description of the four guardian dragons who hibernated above the nest until the conditions were right for hatching. A map just like the one Nathan took from Suzi. All of this had been embedded in an email. The sender's address was a jumble of numbers and letters. Instead of .com or .net, the destination ended in .dmk, whatever that meant.

Nathan joined her at the cave entrance.

"Kang and Suzi were not working alone," Kathy said as she shuffled through the pages. "He might have had a lot of background lore on the dragons of Kilauea, but someone else fed him the very specific information that made freeing them and hatching the nest possible."

"Deputy Director Leister said a lot of the dangerous creatures the National Parks were created to contain have been recently trying to escape. Is it a little too James-Bond-Spectre-like to think that these events are all coordinated?"

"Not after looking at these pages," Kathy said. She looked into the cavern. "Blinded or not, we need to seal that dragon back under Kilauea."

"Lucky us, we have a bomb and a detonator."

"And that will eliminate a lot of evidence we don't want to explain. Now we just need a damn good story to cover the rest."

CHAPTER 40

By the time Kathy and Nathan returned to Kathy's Jeep, the sun had passed apogee. They plugged their dead cell phones into outlets for some power. Both pinged that there were waiting messages. All of them were from the park headquarters number. They looked at each other with dread.

"Looks like the superintendent missed us today," Nathan said.

"No way he couldn't," Kathy said.

"I kind of hoped maybe he'd been too busy, had a meeting in Hilo all day, maybe down with the flu."

Kathy skipped the first three messages and went straight to the fourth one. She pressed play and got a terse message from the superintendent. She was suspended from duty and had to meet him in his office at nine in the morning. She deleted the message and turned to Nathan, who had his ear to his phone. His face fell and he hung up his phone.

"Don't tell me," Kathy said. "You're suspended and the superintendent wants to see you at nine."

"He can totally fire us, right? I mean our secret mission for Deputy Director Leister is secret. She might let us go rather than risk exposing the true story behind the park system, right?"

"She might. But if she does, at least we saved the park, and who knows how many lives."

"Well, yeah, there's that."

When they got back to their quarters, Kathy felt a great sense of relief as she closed the door behind her. Whatever was going to happen to her tomorrow couldn't be worse than what she'd been through the last few days. She couldn't wait to shed her dirty, ragged flight suit and take a steaming hot shower.

But first, she sat down at her computer. She went to her clandestine email account. The usual fifty new spam messages filled her inbox. She began a new email addressed to Victor Moreno. In the body she typed in the prearranged code message for mission complete.

Fantastic weather. Having fun.

She hit send, and hoped that someone at the other end was actually reading these things.

***

The next morning, she and Nathan stood outside Superintendent Butler's office in crisp, clean uniforms. But there was no covering up the plethora of scrapes and bruises the last few days had created. And even with a night to let him heal, Nathan's face looked like he'd spent the day on the beach. His close proximity to the lava flow had given him a little bit of a burn.

"Sleep well?" Kathy said.

"Like Lincoln the night before his assassination," Nathan said. "Which, before you ask me, means no I did not."

Butler looked up to see them in his doorway. "Well, you two do occasionally show up for something. That's refreshing. Get in here."

The two entered and stood in front of the superintendent's desk. Kathy figured there was no point in starting her explanation. He'd be sure to ask for it.

"I don't know what's wrong with you two," Butler said. "You've been classic screwups since you got here. Nothing but trouble. And after I specifically drew the big line in the sand for you, and said miss no interpretives, what happens?"

"We missed interpretives," Nathan said.

"But we have a good reason," Kathy said.

"Shut up," Butler said to Kathy. He turned to Nathan. "The last I heard from you was that there's a fresh lava flow in the Mau Loa restricted area. Visitors report hearing an explosion and you destroy a Park Service vehicle. After the truck gets towed back, you don't even file a report."

Nathan opened his mouth. Butler cut him off with a sweep of his hand.

"And you," Butler said to Kathy. "I don't even know where to start with you. You ignore your schedule. You ignore direct orders from me. It's as if you think you have some work to do more important than running the park."

Kathy would have volunteered a month's pay to be able to tell him as a matter of fact that was true.

"I have no idea how you've managed to stay employed with the Park Service as long as you have," Butler continued. "But my plan today is to rectify that for both of you."

The statement hit Kathy like a hammer. She looked at Nathan. He appeared crestfallen. He hadn't had this dream job of his for even a year, and now he was losing it while he'd done more for the Park Service than any other ranger she knew.

"Or that was my plan," Butler said. "But as I was beginning the termination paperwork, six notifications of transfer came in. They included one each for the both of you. Which is an answer to my prayers, because processing a transfer is no work for me, while processing a termination is a ton of work that would drag on all the way through your unemployment hearing. So as of tomorrow morning, you start being Yellowstone's problem. I'd give the superintendent there a heads up, but Dave Coletta's running the park, and I always thought the guy was a bit of a jerk. So, I'll let him realize what prize packages the two of you are all by himself."

Nathan practically collapsed with relief. Kathy feared that he was going to hug Butler. She had to admit she was certainly happier being transferred than being fired.

"Both of you get the hell out of here and get packed. You're both on a red-eye flight tonight back to the mainland. Movers will ship the rest after you."

Kathy and Nathan managed to control their elation until they got outside.

"As Teddy Roosevelt would say," Nathan said, "just dodged a bullet."

Kathy gave him a quizzical look.

"See, that's funny because in 1912, there was an assassination attempt on President Roosevelt. The bullet pierced the speech in his pocket—"

"Way less funny if you have to explain it, Nathan."

"Totally get it. Just psyched to still be a ranger."

Just as they got back to their quarters, Kathy's phone rang. The name for the caller was Victor Moreno. She didn't have a number programmed in for the alias Victor Moreno. She answered the call.

"Hello?"

"Get someplace where it's safe to talk." It was the gravelly voice of Deputy Director Leister.

Kathy unlocked the door to her quarters and waved Nathan in with her. She locked the door behind them and put the phone on speaker.

"I'm in my quarters," she said. "Nathan is with me."

"I was at Sequoia National Park last night when your message came in that you'd completed the mission. What happened?"

Kathy and Nathan gave her the story of their fight with the Kilauea dragons.

"And you think that the threat is contained?" she said.

"The nest is destroyed," Kathy said. "And the Alika Brotherhood will be collapsing the open tunnels today."

"They can be trusted with this knowledge?"

"Totally," Nathan said. "They've kept incidents far worse a secret for hundreds of years."

"I'm guessing that you engineered our transfers," Kathy said.

"Along with four others to make it look less suspicious," Leister said. "I saw that Butler's search history at work included termination processes and as much background as he could find on the two of you. Looked like you needed to get out of Volcanoes while you could."

"That sure saved us," Nathan said.

"We found something pretty disturbing," Kathy said.

"Like fire-breathing dragons weren't disturbing enough, right?" Nathan said.

Kathy took the printout sheets from Kang's cave out of a drawer and began to take pictures of them. She sent the pictures to the Victor Moreno number she was speaking to.

"Kang didn't come up with this plan on his own. You can see that a lot of the details came from someone else at a web address like I've never seen before."

There was a moment of silence. "Yes. These confirm my worst fears. The release of the creatures the parks have held captive isn't by chance. Someone knows where they are, and what they are. Whoever it is knows more than even I do."

"Who could know more than you do?"

"The only people who did were the band that created the National Parks as our secret line of defense. All were recruited into the OSS in World War II, and none survived. Or so I thought."

"He needs to be stopped," Kathy said, "before he gets people to unleash catastrophes in multiple parks across the country."

"That's why you're going to Yellowstone."

"The first park," Nathan said. "Set aside in 1872. Everything began there."

"As did the shadow leadership that ran the secret mission of the parks. They left everything there when they headed off to World War II, assuming they'd be back to restart the operation. But no one came back."

"And you think whatever records they had would still be there somewhere?" Kathy said.

"They've never been found," Leister said.

"No way records that mega-amazing would be discovered and not make the news," Nathan said.

"We'll start looking," Kathy said.

"Stay in touch through the usual channels."

Leister hung up. Kathy called up her call log. The phone call she'd just completed didn't exist. She checked her address list. No Victor Moreno.

"How in the hell…" she muttered.

Nathan was beaming. "All awesome news today. One: I'm not fired. Two: The next mission is historical research. Three: No giant creatures trying to squash us."

"Don't count on that," Kathy said. "Yellowstone was made a park for a reason. I'll bet we'll find out exactly what that reason was."

AFTERWORD

Dragons. Mythical creatures since the dawn of time. Perhaps inspired by dinosaur bones eroded to the Earth's surface thousands of years ago. We may never know how the idea started. But I can tell you about one that walks the earth today, the one that inspired the dragons of Kilauea.

Komodo dragons are real life bad-ass reptiles. Living in a very restricted set of Asian Pacific islands, the largest recorded specimen reached a length of 10.3 feet (3.13 meters) and weighed 366 pounds (166 kilograms). The fictional dragons in the story were only twice that large.

The dragon's movable intramandibular hinge opens the lower jaw unusually wide, and coupled with an easily expanding stomach, permits an adult to consume up to 80 percent of its own body weight at one time. Tooth serrations catch bits of meat from the Komodo's last meal. This protein-rich residue supports up to sixty different bacterial strains, at least seven of which are highly septic. Infections from the Komodo bite will usually kill in less than a week. Even worse, Komodos have a venom gland in their lower jaw. The venom prevents blood from clotting. So Komodo dragon wounds get infected and they bleed forever. That's a grim prognosis for the victim.

But while my dragons breathed fire, Komodo dragons do not. So they have that in their favor.

One of the things I hope to accomplish with my Kathy West adventures is to inspire a visit to one of our wonderful National Parks, so I try to use as much fact as possible in both the background and the foreground of the stories. Let's see what kind of reality leaked into the fiction.

All the history around the timeline of Volcanoes National Park is true, as is the description of the slow-moving lava activity during eruptions. There have recently been a series of real-life eruptions that in the story I attributed to Suzi and Kang. As I was finishing this book, they appear to have subsided. For now. But many features at the park have been closed temporarily for safety reasons.

And those lava tubes? Definitely real things. You can explore the Thurston Lava Tube in the park with no more caving gear than a flashlight. But the ones out in the wilds are as dangerous and unpredictable as the ones portrayed in the book. Do not go wandering into one looking for dragons.

Kilauea Military Camp is a real place, and the infantry unit mentioned was the first group of soldiers to set up camp there. If you are active duty U.S. military or a U.S. military veteran, you are eligible to book a cabin there. If you qualify and are going to the Big Island, you must stay there at least a few nights. The accommodations are rustic but in no way make you rough it, and the entire vibe of the place makes you swear you are hearing Big Band music in the background.

Kathy finds the ruins of a pulu factory in the wilds of the park. This was a real industry in the 18th century, but it died out as described, not due to dragon attacks. Imagine having your pillow stuffed with Hawaiian ferns? How exotic.

The Alika Brotherhood is pure fiction, but the Native Hawaiian spirit to protect the island is a real and powerful thing. Your visit to the island is incomplete if you don't check out the many different museums and historic sites celebrating the Hawaiian people and their culture.

Part of Kang's motivation is the death of his father trying to sabotage Kilauea. An event similar to the one described actually happened in 2008, when the first explosion in Halema'uma'u crater since 1924 occurred. Debris from the huge explosion was scattered over an area of 74 acres. Debris covered part of Crater Rim Drive and damaged Halema'uma'u Overlook. No lava was released, so scientists attributed it to an accumulation of natural gasses. It definitely wasn't caused by a crazed man with a homemade bomb.

Our National Park system is like a string of diamonds, each one different and each one beautiful. Volcanoes National Park is a must-do experience. I have been there several times and it never fails to amaze. Put it on your bucket list. I promise it will be dragon-free.

A big thanks to real-life National Park Service rangers Denise Ratajczak and Maria Thomson who were kind enough to answer a ton of questions about the Park Service during the 2019 Miami Book Fair.

And then there are my faithful beta readers Donna Fitzpatrick, Deb DeAlteriis, Jonathan Moore, and Teresa Robeson who took the first version of this story and swept up all the crumbs and straightened the linen to make it something worthy of offering to you amazing readers.

Kathy and Nathan are off to Yellowstone, due a break in the action after everything they endured in Hawaii. Will they find it? Something tells me there's another adventure awaiting them there. I'll find out soon enough and let you know.

Russell James
June 2020

Made in the USA
Las Vegas, NV
11 February 2022

43730146R00089